THE HORN'S HOAX

The Forbidden Instrument

Héctor Cantú Kalifa

ACKNOWLEDGE

I dedicate this book to the following people:

My wife, Paulina, because I always had her support. As a father of four young children, she found me time and space to write. She inspired me and encouraged me to improve the novel. Without her support and positivity, this book would not be the same.

My children, because the idea for the book came from how I play with them. And because they teach me how to be a better father. They were the reason to create this story, and their creativity and imagination inspired me. They are my blessing; I would not have written this book if they hadn't played with me. **A special dedication to them.**

My parents, for the lessons and values I received from them. They have taught me to be honest with others and myself. To have a sense of responsibility for my doings. And especially to love and respect others, treating everyone the way you want to be treated. They made sure I always had the best. Thanks for the support and effort.

Last, I would like to thank my editors who helped improve my writing and my ideas, and to make this book the best it could be. And to the beta readers who took the time to read and give their comments.

PROLOGUE

Blue energy sparked through the black circle in the sky as a body fell, smashing the ground with a thud. The portal vanished.

The brother rapidly stood up. "No, no, no, — Why? What the hell have you *done*?" he howled to himself, searching for the portal. He paced side to side, hands wringing. *This can't be happening. This can't be happening,* he kept thinking. A lump formed in his gut, and his breath quickened. The more he thought about it, the more his heart raced. The tension moved through his chest, up his throat, until he unleashed a scream of fury.

It was partly his fault. He could've pulled his brother inside the portal.

He hesitated. To his left, a swirl of dust. To his right, a rolling bush. "Where am I?" he asked out loud. He was standing on a road, alone in a desert, clutching a small, strange animal horn.

"*Damn* it," he yowled, staring at the horn. He raised his arm to toss it away; then, a thought struck him. He ground his teeth in frustration because he couldn't get rid of it—it was the only way to get back to the portal.

He clenched the horn, face reddened in anger, and yelled, "Itenelum, Dantus." He repeated, "Itenelum, Dantus."

Nothing. The horn wasn't activating.

He headed down the road. The radiant sun beat down. He hoped to return to where he had suffered the strangest experience he'd ever had.

In the distance, metal clattered. He raised his burned face, eyes squinting at the smudge on the horizon, and eyed a billboard. The advertisement promised *Coffee Cheer, Morning Cheers.*

He gasped, widening his eyes. "The sign."

He hastened to the billboard, looking for the dirt road. He stopped, and his face dropped again. No dirt road, only bushes. He sprinted to the bushes and yanked several from the ground. "Where is the road?"

Could he get back to the cabin? There was no dirt road to lead him.

He walked a few paces away from the bushes, his hands dirty and bleeding. Now he thought of getting home. But had his family survived? He walked toward his house, his weary feet dragging on the ground.

He recalled his experience and sensed ominous times ahead. As if the ones he'd already lived through weren't enough.

Soon, the hum of a motor approached as an old pickup drove towards him. *Finally.* Covered in dust, he waved the vehicle down as he tucked the horn in his jacket.

The driver squinted at him, then shrugged and slowed to a halt. He backed up and addressed the brother. The driver was bald, with wrinkles on his forehead and a long white beard.

At the obvious question he wanted to answer, *I just waved my hand for no reason.* Instead, he said, "Yes, please. I have been walking for hours and have no cell phone."

"Where're you headed?"

Anywhere out of here, the brother thought. "Near Austin," he said with a forced smile.

"Hop in. I'm going that way."

"Thank you very much, sir."

The clock on the dashboard flashed a useless twelve o'clock, and the radio was off. The brother hesitated to ask about the date; a scruffy guy on the side of the road asking that sounded normal, right? He remained silent.

The driver held a one-sided conversation that the brother mostly ignored. He stared out the window, his hand on the horn in his pocket and his mind on the experience before the black hole. The driver kept chattering.

When they finally arrived at the outskirts of Austin, he asked the driver to drop him off near his house. He stepped out and, embarrassedly, offered only a thank-you. He had no money.

He hesitated a second in trepidation after the pickup left him, then rushed toward home.

There were no cars in the house.

"Oh, *no,*" he wailed. He feared death had visited his family.

The brother approached the door and rang the bell. No one answered. He searched for the hidden key below the flowerpot—it was still there—and went inside.

"Mom? Maya? Are you here?"

No one answered. He glanced around and sighed, smiling. He saw a picture of them. They still lived in the house.

He needed to figure out the date. He hurried to a laptop, opened it, and waited for it to boot up.

CHAPTER 1
THE UNEXPECTED VACATIONS

It was a lovely summer evening when Henry arrived home for the day. Unfortunately, the weather was at odds with his mood.

He walked in the door with his black hair disheveled, his tie loosened, and his shirt untucked and half-unbuttoned. His green eyes were swollen with exhaustion.

"You look dreadful," said his mother, Susan, as she washed the dishes.

He gasped in pain, less physical and more mental. "It's just work, and Robert," he complained.

"Stop with that," Susan said. "Robert is not who you assume he is."

"How would you know, Mom? Dad hated him almost as much as I hate this job."

"Hated? You know they were friends, right?"

"You never saw them at work. And before Dad … *you know*. They argued a lot since they hired me as an intern."

"Coworkers can argue. And what would your father

think about his son detesting the company he worked for his entire life?"

"I don't know. But every day I go to Vultock, it just reminds me about what happened to him…" Henry paused to swallow. "— and his disappearance." The tears he held back turned his eyes bloodshot.

Susan left the dishes, approached, and hugged him. "You need to let out your feelings, Henry. It's been, what, two months since your father disappeared? Have you cried?"

"You can't ask me that, Mom. Everyone has their own process of grieving. Besides, I need to be strong for Moris and Maya," his voice quavered.

"Oh Henry, that doesn't make you strong. It doesn't matter if you are sixteen or sixty; you can cry. Otherwise, the grief will consume you, and you'll lose control of yourself. But for now, you can find another job if it would make you feel better."

"No. Now that it's a summer job, I have full time to find out what happened to Dad and how Robert's involved."

Robert and his Dad, Kevin, worked together at Vultock enterprise long before Kevin disappeared.

"C'mon, Henry. You can't say he's involved if you haven't found proof."

"I'm working on it. Meanwhile, I've got to pretend I like him." Henry added, "You know the last conversation I had with Dad, he seemed upset and said he was leaving Robert's department. Everyone knew about the growing dislike between them."

"Remember that your father trusted him." Susan looked

him over and changed the topic. "But for now, go get cleaned up. Your siblings are waiting for you to play The Game."

Moris and Maya came running down the stairs and greeted him with big hugs. "Henry! Henry! Come and play The Universe Game," Moris begged, gazing up at him with pleading eyes.

"Yeah, let's travel in the blanket fort like we used to play with Dad," said Maya.

Now sixteen, Henry wanted his siblings to have the same experiences of living with Dad. They wouldn't be interested in playing much longer. Maya, at twelve, was almost done. Moris was only a year younger but more fanciful and might play longer.

Henry's nose scrunched. "You both stink." He made his voice hoarse, imitating Dad. "Take a bath and brush your teeth. Then we play until ten."

"Let's see who finishes first," Moris said and raced off to complete his tasks.

Not even four minutes passed before the kids rushed back. Moris started to speak, "Let's—"

Susan frowned. "Really, that fast?"

Moris scampered with his sister and jumped onto the big bed to play The Game. Henry sighed, turned to his mother, and gave a weary look. Susan shrugged and beamed. He headed to the bedroom and stopped in the doorway, staring at the bed. He saw himself playing with his Dad when he was a kid. A flashback that he always tried to avoid. Tears swelled in his eyes. *Be strong,* he thought as he held the sob in his stomach.

The kids scrambled under the bed sheet.

"It's my turn to go first," Maya said.

"Why you first?" Moris asked.

"You were first the last time."

"She's right, Moris," Henry said. "She goes first."

Henry joined them, and Maya started shaking the bed sheet. She said, "This spaceship wants to go to Dinosaur World."

The kids made a raspy sound, trembling their body as if the bed flew through different dimensions until they arrived at Dinosaur World. They dashed out of the room and Henry roared, chasing his siblings around the house with a pillow to fight.

Susan watched Henry hunting after them. She grinned, and a tear fell to the floor. For this moment, happiness reigned in the house. They all needed it—that's why Henry played, even though it crushed his heart.

Henry caught Maya, locked her, and hit her with the pillow. She laughed. He then did the same to Moris.

"Now it's my turn to choose the Universe," Moris said, and they trooped back to the bed.

Suddenly, the door of the room slammed. The three of them gasped, startled.

"What was that?" asked Maya.

"Sorry, it was me again," said Moris.

Maya giggled. "I thought your power was running super fast."

"It really was me. I stared at the door and shut it with my eyes."

"You're obsessed with magic, Moris," Maya said.

"If it can bring back Dad, then yes. I'm obsessed."

"Henry, are you sure he's eleven?" asked Maya, taunting.

Henry chuckled. "Are you sure you're twelve?"

Maya was different too but in another way. Her gift was superior intelligence.

Henry stood up, went to the window, and closed it. He said no word of it.

"You see, it was the wind," said Maya.

"Does it matter?" asked Henry, returning to the bed. "Moris, what world do you want to travel to?"

"I want Heroes World."

They performed the same ritual, rubbing the bed sheet and trembling their bodies as they flew to it. Moris darted off with a zoom sound as fast as he could.

"Look, it's the Flash," Maya taunted, rolling her eyes as she got off the bed.

"Stop Maya, you picked the last world," said Henry.

"I'm bored with this one," she replied.

Maybe they had less time with Maya than Henry had thought. He got closer and said in a low voice, "Do it for Moris. Do it for Dad."

Maya sighed, then flexed her arm muscles. "I'm Captain Marvel," she announced, and punched Henry in the chest.

Henry groaned and stood up, towering over her. "You can't hurt Hulk."

Maya's eyes widened, and she ran out of the room with a yell.

Henry chased them around the house.

On the run, Maya tripped on a step and fell. Gripping her knee, she started to cry. Henry hurried over and examined the injury. It didn't seem bad. He bent and kissed the wound. "My strength is yours," he said, just as Dad did when someone got hurt.

At these familiar words, Maya tears turned to sobbing.

Henry was stoic, like always. He swallowed the lump in his throat and hugged her in silence.

The ceiling light blinked right as a picture on the wall of Mom and Dad rattled. The kids didn't notice, but Henry did. He frowned, unsettled. *Was it Dad's ghost?* After his father disappeared, he has experienced paranormal events.

Susan came up the stairs, Moris in tow, to check on the crying.

"They miss Dad," Henry said, low and sad.

"We all miss him," Susan said tenderly, stroking the kids' hair. "Remember that he's always with you, in your—"

"How? He's dead," Maya said from her cocoon in Henry's arms.

"You don't know that," howled Moris. "He just disappeared."

They argued, and Maya pushed her little brother. The ceiling lamps blinked repeatedly, longer than the last time. Everyone watched. *BOOM!* The light bulb exploded.

They yelped in fright.

"It's okay," Susan assured them. "It's only a power surge."

"No, it was Dad saying hello, or … or scolding us," said Moris.

"How's that even possible?" asked Maya.

"Maybe his spirit came and expressed himself."

"Spirit?" Maya laughed.

"C'mon kids. Don't start. Go to bed; it's ten o'clock." Susan hustled the protesting children to their room.

Later, after Henry had made himself dinner and the kids were asleep, Susan rejoined him in the kitchen. He asked, "How was your day, Mom?"

"Well," she said in a quiet voice as she sat beside Henry, "the school called today. They're worried about Moris. He's been alone in class and recess. And Maya has been more defiant with her teachers."

Henry hesitated. "I don't know what to say."

"You don't need to say anything." She patted his hand. "Anyway, thank you for asking. I'm gonna head to bed; I'm very tired." She stood up and kissed Henry on the forehead.

***

Henry frowned. He didn't recognize the large, old rustic cabin surrounded by trees before him. He glanced around, and haze covered the forest.

Where am I?

Two people exited in a hurry. One was short and bald, dressed in scuba gear with a gold gauntlet wristband and an unfamiliar type of helmet. The other one was normal-sized, dressed all in black, and wore a dark trench coat.

Who are they?

Henry followed the people until a scream echoed from afar. He twisted around, searching for the yell.

What's that?

The yelling got louder and louder. Henry walked toward the woods, following the noise. The haze covered his sight, and the screams were more intense. He shivered but kept moving. Suddenly, the person in the black trench coat came out of nowhere with sparks in his fist.

Henry jerked awake in bed, gasping. The clock said *6:56 a.m.* The screaming continued. "What the hell," he groaned. He put on the slippers and stood up, eyes half-opened. He followed the shouting downstairs, where his siblings were arguing.

"I called for the bread first," said Maya.

"I don't care. I want some too," said Moris.

"Why don't you use your magic and make some appear?" scoffed Maya.

Henry looked around for his mother. "Mom!"

The kids kept bickering.

"Hey! What the heck?" Henry scowled. "It's seven a.m., and you're already fighting. Stop Moris; she grabbed it first. Find something else."

"No! Why her?"

"It's too early to fight for stupid bread. Eat something else."

Henry heard footsteps coming downstairs. *Finally, Mom.* He sighed in relief.

"Henry? Can you take the kids to school? Today is their last day." Susan said hastily as she took the car keys.

Henry's face dropped again. "Do I have a choice?"

"No, I need to be at work in thirty minutes. I have early client appointments."

"Okay. I'm taking a bath," Henry said as he went back to his room.

"Kids, no fighting. Share the bread. Then get ready for school." Her harsh voice made them agree. "I'll buy groceries later."

A few minutes later, Henry came down dressed. "Maya, Moris, let's go. Get in the car." Henry hastened to the car. The kids' pace was slow. So he shouted, desperately, "Hurry up, I need to be at work,"

The kids hurried to the back seat. Entering, Moris grabbed a bow and a steel arrow that was in the car. "Henry, can you teach me archery?"

"No. Leave the arrow."

"Why not? Dad taught you when you were my age."

Maya chuckled. "You don't know how to throw a ball, and you want to throw an arrow?"

"That has nothing to do with it," said Moris.

"*Stop*," Henry rasped. "No more talking."

A silence emerged for a moment.

After Henry relaxed, Moris asked, "Henry? Are we going on vacation like all summers?"

"Yes, please," said Maya. "That would be awesome."

Henry glanced at them in the rearview mirror. "I don't think so. I have a lot of work."

"Aww," both lamented at the same time.

"Hey Moris," said Maya. "Why don't we travel with your powers?" She cackled at her own joke.

"I will. But I'm not taking you."

"Stop fighting!" Henry snapped and hit the steering wheel.

The kids froze, startled. "Are you okay, Henry?" Moris asked.

"That's enough with you two. Why do you always fight so much?"

"What happened to you?" asked Maya back.

"Don't answer with another question," said Henry.

"She's right, Henry," said Moris. "You've been different since Dad disappeared."

"We've all been different. The school called Mom about you two."

"But you more. And Maya and me, we're just playing, not fighting."

Henry recalled his mother saying: *grief will consume you.* He shook off his bad temper and gave up arguing. They were right, and he knew it. Maybe Mom had spoken the truth—holding his emotions had weakened him.

They arrived at school. Before going in, Maya turned to him. "Henry," she said in a tender voice. "You don't have to be brave for us."

Henry snorted in silence. *This girl is really something.* "Bye Maya." he said. He watched Moris and Maya walking beside one another. *Maybe they can get along,* he thought. Then Moris pushed Maya. *Maybe not.*

The dash clock read eight a.m; he was almost late for a meeting. He drove quickly across town, parked the car in the parking lot beside the Vultock building, and hurried inside.

Entering the lobby, the receptionist greeted him, "Good morning, Henry."

"Morning, Raquel," he replied as he breezed past.

"I want to thank you for what your father did for me."

Henry frowned and turned back. "What?"

"His herbal medicine cured my terminal cancer."

"Glad to hear it. I've got to go, I'm running late."

He entered the elevator. As the doors closed, her words hit him. *Herbal medicine? Cure her? What was she talking about?* The elevator opened on his floor, and there was his co-worker and friend, passing by with his coffee. "Hey Tomas, has the meeting started?"

"You got lucky; it's cancelled."

Henry sighed in relief. "Well then, I'm gonna grab a coffee."

"Hey, hey," Tomas stopped him and whispered, "Did John accomplish the thing?"

Henry hesitated, glanced around them before answering. "He finished late, but yes."

"Have you looked at it?"

"Not yet; I need my coffee first."

"Tell me what you find."

"Will do."

Henry grabbed his coffee and sat down at his desk. He turned on the computer and opened the software John had installed. It connected to Robert's computer. The first thing Henry did was search Robert's emails. He read many of the emails between Robert and his father. He started from a year ago and read each one. One email a month before his Dad disappeared said:

Kevin,

Listen to me, stop what you're doing. I'm warning you.
There will be consequences, and you have a family.
Think about it.
P.S. I'll not warn you again.

Henry's eyes widened. He kept reading, trying to figure out what his Dad was doing or why he was threatened. He found nothing else in Robert's emails. Yet, this was proof Robert knew something. He entered the folders on Robert's hard drive and clicked one by one. One folder was named Bitraculus. *An odd name,* he thought. He clicked on it, but it was encrypted. His attempts to crack the password all failed.

"Henry?"

Henry jerked and closed the software. Robert himself stood in front of him. The fellow had a wrinkled, angry face, always scowling, and his eyes like they were depressed all the time. "Do you have the report on the stone we found under the sea?" Robert asked.

"Not yet. I just received the results. Let me work on it."

"I thought they gave the data to you yesterday."

"I had problems accessing it and they had to send it again."

"I want it today."

"Yes, sir. You'll have it this afternoon."

Henry stopped investigating Robert's emails and went back to his real job.

Vultock was an artificial intelligence enterprise and one

business unit specialized in archaeology. They could trace artifacts and fossils, treasures and know their age and where they came from. Henry's responsibility was to summarize and present the results of the archaeological artifacts studied.

It took all day and into the evening, but Henry finished the report and sent it off to Robert. He continued his investigation on Robert, but he got stuck in the encrypted folder. He groaned, his eyes red for the computer screen. The clock said eleven p.m. and he was tired.

Henry got up, closed the computer screen, and went for the car. He drove back home, and the thought of Robert's email couldn't get off his mind. *What does Robert meant when he wrote: 'there will be consequences'?* He entered the house, and there was his mother, sitting at the dinner table, her hands wrapped around a cup of tea. She seemed concerned.

Henry sat down with her. "Hi Mom, how was your day?"

Susan sipped the tea and replied with a dubious face, "I think they liked one of the houses I showed them."

Henry squeezed her shoulder. "You'll close a deal. You're the best, Mom."

Susan smiled. "And how was your day?"

Henry hesitated, unsure whether to tell her about the email he found. He remembered how Susan felt about Robert and decided he needed more proof. "It was tiring like every other day recently."

"You didn't complain when you started working there."

"I liked it better when Dad was there."

"You need to get out with your friends, invite a girl to dinner. You have done nothing fun since your father disappeared."

"I'd love to do that, Mom. I'm exhausted from work. There's twenty times the number of artifacts to process now."

Susan hesitated. "You know that any other time, I'd ask you to stop working, right?"

Henry nodded and held her hand. "Don't worry, Mom. I know we need the money."

Susan beamed, a tear slipping down her cheek. Her voice quavered, "Thank you."

Henry stood up, kissed his mother on the cheek, and said, "Goodnight, Mom."

"Aren't you gonna eat?"

"I'm not hungry; I'd rather sleep."

Up in his room, took a photo frame of him and his father playing archery. He paused to look and sighed. He went to bed, took out his cellphone, and killed some time on social media. He was too wired to sleep yet. Pictures of his friends at a house party, others dancing, scrolled on his screen. A girl he liked had uploaded a party photo only minutes ago. He tapped the heart icon below the picture; seconds later, she sent a message: "Join us!"

Henry was tempted. He reread the message several times, looked at the picture once more; instead, he turned off his phone and went to sleep.

***

Henry woke the next morning earlier than normal. He grabbed a bagel and left for work. At the first traffic light, he passed a car with an advertisement for a rustic cabin surrounded by a verdant forest. Henry frowned; his eyes followed the picture. The car behind him honked, and he jerked his attention back to the road.

Henry arrived at Vultock and parked in his usual spot. Climbing the front steps of the building, he caught from the corner of his eye a billboard flashing the same rustic cabin. He halted and stared at it, raising one brow. Henry thought it looked very familiar, but he can't place his finger on it. The digital image flipped to the next ad. Henry shook it off and entered the building. Inside, he went straight for a morning coffee.

"What happened?" asked Tomas, after seeing Henry's haggard face. He stirred his own coffee with a spoon.

"The weirdest thing happened this — never mind. I'm just tired of working with Robert. I think I'm gonna quit."

"You know you won't. You are so close to discovering the truth. Have you looked at his emails?"

Henry snorted. "He is involved. Last email I read, Robert threatened my Dad with 'consequences', but it didn't say why or what. Every time I see that bastard, I want to punch him in the face."

"Shh," Tomas hissed, staring behind Henry.

Henry whirled around. Robert was ten feet away, eyeing him. Henry's pulse quickened. Had he overheard anything? Was Henry going to get fired? Even though he hated his job, he couldn't be fired. All the evidence about his father's disappearance was here at the company.

Robert walked away.

Henry sighed. "Do you think he heard me?"

"I don't know. Pray he didn't."

"Let me get back to work."

"Work as in actual work, or work as in *work?*" Tomas asked with a wink.

Henry smirked and headed to his desk.

An hour later, Robert phoned Henry. "Come to my office, now, please." And with that, the line went dead.

Henry froze for a second, then slid the chair back and stood up. He walked down the long hallway, shivering. *Be calm,* he repeated under his breath as his chest tightened. His hands wouldn't stop wringing. Had Robert heard him earlier?

He entered the office, and Robert didn't mince words. "Henry, I've noticed you acting strangely. And you look dreadful today."

Henry loosened. He could handle a regular Robert chewing out. If he'd been overheard with Tomas, Robert would've just fired him. Henry pulled a sadden face. "Well, what can I say? I miss my father," his voice was low.

"Take some days off."

Henry frowned. *Is this a trick?*

"How am I supposed to take time off now?" he asked, confused. They had a huge workload and there'd been layoffs. Taking a vacation would be seen as irresponsible.

Robert said, "I already filed the paperwork for you, starting tomorrow. Take it as paid time off and relax with your family."

Henry doubted his boss's motives. Robert was up to something. Did he know Henry was getting closer to finding the truth?

Nevertheless, the prospect of a break was enticing.

"Well then. Thank you very much, Robert," Henry said.

So Henry wasn't fired—for now. He headed back to his desk, opened the laptop, and connected to Robert's hard drive.

Henry goes straight to the *Bitraculus* folder. He double-clicked it and tried again to guess the password. *What does Bitraculus mean?* He huffed and put the idea aside; there were too many tasks to finish before he left for the week.

Many hours later, the clock on the wall marked nine forty-five p.m. Almost bedtime for his siblings. He left work and drove home, eager to tell his family the news in person. He would want to see Moris and Maya's reaction.

As he opened the front door of his house, he heard his mother saying, "*Good night,*" while she closed the upstairs bedroom door. He went to the kitchen.

He opened the fridge and took the first leftovers he could find. Eating them cold, he opened his laptop and began researching for places to visit.

The first result was a beach in Cancun. Too expensive for them. He scrolled through downhill skiing, a ranch, hiking the mountains, a fishing trip. Then, an advertisement with a promotion for a cabin emerged. Henry stopped and stared at it. He shivered. It was the same rustic cabin he'd seen on the car this morning and on the electronic billboard—and in his dream. Was this a joke? He studied it and, as the temptation grew, he clicked on it.

Photos of a picturesque cabin in a forest and families having fun appeared on his screen. He had a strong sense of *déjà vu.*

"Mom?" yelled Henry. "Come here, please. I want you

to see a cabin that looks amazing."

"Don't yell," Susan hollered back.

Henry half-smirked, half-smiled. "You're yelling at me not to yell."

Susan came down the stairs. "Why do you want me to see a cabin?"

"They gave me a week's vacation."

"Really? That's strange."

"Well…" Henry paused, ashamed at what he would say next. "Robert gave me a week to spend time together."

"You see. I told you, he's not bad," Susan said.

Henry snorted and then said, "I found this two-story cabin in a forest. It has three bedrooms."

"Can we afford it?"

"We can. It has a special discount."

"Let me see." She peered over his shoulder, looking at the cabin photos. "It says the weather is semi-cold … in summer?"

"Maybe at night. I don't know."

"Seems like a good choice … Let me see other options."

Henry showed Susan the search results. "Too expensive…" she kept scrolling. "Not for kids … bad reviews … not available. Well, the cabin is the right choice. You have my blessing."

Henry said, "It's not quite perfect. It says the caretakers are an elderly couple and are two miles away from the cabin. So, if we need anything in the cabin, it's a long way to them."

"We should be fine; I don't think we'd need them."

Henry made the reservation. He received a confirmation email with instructions, directions to the cabin, and a map of the forest.

CHAPTER 2
THE RUSTIC CABIN

"What are you still doing here?" Moris asked as Henry dumped another bag on the pile of luggage… "Are those magic bags from another universe?"

The boy always tried to find something magical in his surroundings.

"Yes, brother," Maya replied, tired of Moris's obsession with magic. "Be careful. If you open one, it may have a magic portal."

Maya had been rougher on Moris after their Dad disappeared. Perhaps it was her way of expressing her sadness. As for Moris, well, he forced himself to believe in magic. It was his way of getting away from his emotions. And for Henry, his humor had evaporated.

"Are we really going on vacation?" Maya asked, a hopeful smile on her face.

"Yes," Susan replied, "I rented—"

Henry cleared his throat.

"—Your brother and I rented a cabin in a forest. Won't that be fun?"

The kids' smiles faded.

Maya asked, "Why a forest instead of Disney World or Universal Studios, like we always do? We just want to have fun, not a random cabin."

Henry looked at Susan, clueless about how to respond.

Susan mumbled, "You'll have lots of space to play in the woods."

"Because we've never gone to forest World," Henry said, jumping into the conversation. He leaned over close to their faces and, in an ominous voice, added, "the legend says whoever goes there might find magic." His voice returned to normal. "But if we don't go, we'll never know."

Moris's smile came back, and Maya huffed.

"Don't scoff," Henry said to Maya, then continued with the same dark voice. "It's said the forest World has rare and supernatural creatures. And it's full of magical trees, rivers, caves and birds."

"Henry," said Susan with a shift smile. "If they don't want to go, we can leave them with your aunt Emma."

"No!" Moris cried. "I want to see real magic in the Forest."

Maya snorted in disgust before agreeing. Henry smiled to himself; he knew Maya wouldn't stay alone with their aunt; she was mean.

Henry packed their luggage into the car and the food for the week.

"Henry, take the keys," said Susan as she tossed them to Henry. "You know I don't like to drive."

Henry got behind the wheel, opened the GPS on his phone, and clicked the search button.

He frowned.

"What's the matter, Henry?" Susan asked.

"It doesn't appear on the GPS."

"Let me see." Susan took his phone.

"I know how to handle a GPS app, Mom."

"Well, you're right. It doesn't show the location."

Henry rolled his eyes.

"By any chance, did you print the map?" Susan asked.

"Yes, it came with the instructions." He waved the paper at her.

She smiled. "Just like the old days."

Henry passed the map to Susan. "On the back is the map inside the forest and the list of activities."

"Good. I'll have a look at it."

***

Driving down the road, they passed a billboard for coffee with a caption: *Coffee Cheer, Morning Cheers.* It stood on the lonely corner of a dirt road.

"Turn here," said Susan.

The car lurched across the dirt. The land grew dusty and barren, and the sky cloudy.

After an especially large bump in the road, the air conditioner cut out. Moris attempted to roll down the window for some relief, but it also jammed. Not even his nose could fit.

Maya whined, "Why are we going to the forest?"

Regret stirred in Henry's mind, but he kept silent. He looked at his mother, and she grimaced.

Passing the bumpy road, Susan said to her children, "Go to sleep; we'll wake you when we get there."

Soon, two desert mountains lay ahead. The road sliced narrowly between them. Henry slowed and made the turn between the mountains.

A chilly breeze blew from the brief space of Moris's window. The sky cleared, lush trees emerged, and colorful flowers lined the road. Enormous and dynamic mountains loomed around them, all reminding Henry of various shapes: a turtle shell, a crocodile, a trunk of an elephant, and many others.

Henry and Susan gawked.

"Look, wake up, we're entering the forest World," said Henry.

Susan reached back and shook each of the children so they wouldn't miss the view.

Moris woke first. "Wow, we are definitely in the forest World," he said as he glanced.

Maya awoke with tears streaming down her face.

"What is it, Maya?" asked her mom.

"I saw Dad," said Maya with a cracked voice.

"You dreamed about him?"

"No … well … Yes, but it felt real like I really saw him."

"That's called a lucid dream," Susan said. "And they often feel real."

In an instant, the car clock started going crazy; numbers kept flickering.

From the corner of his eyes, Henry glimpsed at it. "What the—" He tapped the clock. First softly, then hard.

Susan frowned. She glanced at her watch, and the clock hands there circled frenetically. "Where are we?"

Up ahead, a rusty steel gate blocked the road. Tree branches covered most of it, except for a symbol in the center.

The cabin entrance.

"What's that?" Moris asked, pointing to the symbol.

"I don't know," Susan said.

Henry stepped out of the car and crept to the gate. The logo featured a round figure as a stone and within, a tilted sword, a crossing spear, two antelope-like horns, and two gauntlet wristbands. The left horn pointed down, the right horn faced up. He cautiously touched it.

The gate opened with a creak, and the symbol lit up. He shivered. A cabin not on the GPS maps. Crazy weather. Insane clocks. And an old creaky gate.

Henry hurried back to the car. He kept his face calm for the kids. Shutting the door, he took a deep breath. *It was nothing,* he thought.

A long road led from the gate to the cabin. Moris tried to roll down the car window—this time it worked—and stuck his head out like a dog. The 'forest world' emerged as they progressed.

Animals appeared, lakes bordered the road, colorful birds flew in the air, deer with huge antlers jumped around, white horses running, dolphins jumping while sea-turtles walked on a lake—Henry had no idea how that's possible—and more amazing animals.

"Look, seahorses on the top of the water," said Susan, amazed.

"I see, that's so cool. They are huge and bizarre," replied Maya, her voice amazed.

Moris taunted her, "*Ahh,* now you believe in the forest World?"

Maya's mouth stayed shut.

Henry's face looked anxious. He turned to Susan, her eyes wide as she watched the weirdness of the forest.

"How did you find this place?" she asked him.

"Don't know, it found me," Henry said. "There were ads all over the place."

"It looks like we made the right choice. The forest looks amazing and peaceful."

After several minutes of driving and enjoying the view, a large, old, rustic cabin of cracked wood appeared before them.

"How can such a beautiful place have a cabin like *this*?" Susan added. "This makes no sense. In the pictures we saw, it showed a beautiful cabin."

Henry stared at the cabin and mused to himself; *This is the dream cabin.* He got out of the car and pulled out his cell phone, groaning at the lack of signal.

"Henry," his mom said, stepping out. "You said you wanted to spend some quality time with your family, so no distractions for us. Leave your cell phone in the car."

Henry gave a sigh.

The kids burst out of the car and looked around the forest. Their eyes couldn't hide their enjoyment. The adults approached the cabin before unloading the car.

Susan opened the door, and to her surprise, the cabin was

clean and beautiful. The cushions were new, the kitchen drawers shone, and the fridge matched the kitchen design.

"Don't judge a book by its cover," Susan said. "Kids? Help me bring your luggage and groceries. Chop Chop!" She clapped her hands.

Maya and Moris didn't move.

"What?" Susan asked. "Why are you not moving?"

"I'm tired," moaned Maya.

Henry walked over to Maya and said, "Stop whining, girl." He grabbed his phone and put some music on. "Dance while you work." Henry started doing a silly dance; he opened his arms, waved them, and howled as he jumped.

Moris and Maya watched, stared at each other, and laughed. Their humor changed, and they went to unload the car.

Susan went upstairs to leave the luggage. As she looked at Henry's room, the corner of her eye caught a movement on the bed. She yelped, paused a moment, and squinted at it. Had the bed itself shaken? Susan couldn't tell if she was going crazy or just tired. She entered and stared at the piece of furniture. It had a black headboard carved like a spider web. There were also symbols etched into the wood. She touched the frame. Were these symbols part of the design? The need to unload their belongings before dark forced her back to work.

Soon they finished everything, the family collapsed in a tired heap on the couch. As one, they all sighed.

After an interval of quiet, Susan sat forward and asked, "Who's going to make dinner?"

The siblings rolled their eyes.

"Are you making jokes, Mom?" Henry asked.

Susan snorted, stood up, and went to the kitchen.

"I'm bored," Maya announced.

"I brought games," said Susan. "They're inside my luggage."

"I wanna play cards," Moris said as he ran for them.

Moris shuffled the cards and said to Maya, "Pick one card."

Maya grabbed one.

"Okay, show it to Henry and hide it away."

Maya did, and Moris closed his eyes.

"What are you doing?" asked Maya.

"Shh," hissed Moris, "Think about your card."

"Okay…"

Moris then touched Maya's head.

Maya frowned.

Seconds later, Moris hummed. "I can sense your card. Your card is … three of spades."

Henry and Maya looked at each other and guffawed.

"No," said Maya, with glee. "King of hearts." She showed the card to Moris.

Moris's face dropped, and he set the deck of cards on the table.

Henry tried to comfort him. "Hey Moris, you'll learn to be a magician. Don't worry."

"Dinner's ready," Susan cut in. She set a plate of sandwiches on the table.

Susan plated her food and sat down. The others joined. "It's so nice to have a peaceful dinner. No cellphone, no TV, no distraction, only us."

Henry hesitated. "I don't think we have ever had that. Dad would have loved it."

"Yeah, I know," said Susan. "Your Dad just wanted you to live peacefully; that's why he never told you—" Susan paused and shut her mouth.

"Told us what, Mom?" asked Maya.

Susan said, "Nothing. Never mind." She took another bite of her sandwich.

"Never mind?" said Henry. "Dad never told us what? You can't say something like that halfway. Finish the sentence."

"He never … told you he wanted to leave the city," replied Susan.

Henry grimaced. "I don't think that's what you were going to say."

"Your father never wanted to live in the big city."

"Yeah, right, and we just work in the city. I don't believe you, and I think you're hiding something."

"Believe what you want," said Susan, and turned her attention to the kids. "When you finish, take the plates to the sink."

After dinner, they did as told.

"Henry, let's play The Universe Game," Moris suggested.

"I wanna play too; there's nothing else to do," Maya said. "We've got time to play. It's not even ten yet."

Henry gave a weary sigh. The dark circles under his eyes said to the world, 'please let me rest'.

"Kids," Susan said, "let your brother rest for tonight." She stroked Henry's shoulder.

He said, "Tomorrow, I promise we'll play. Even if it's after ten o'clock."

"Really?" Moris and Maya said as one.

"Promise."

Susan stayed with the kids and played cards. Henry did the dishes. After, he grabbed his luggage and went to his room for the first time.

Henry eyed the strange headboard. It shook. "What the—?" he said, craning his neck. He blinked twice, not sure if he'd really seen it trembling.

I need sleep, he thought.

CHAPTER 3
THE NEW BEGINNING

"Morning kids," Susan said the next day. "Are you ready for today? Breakfast is outside on the picnic table. There are fruits and bagels."

"Ready for what?" asked Maya.

Henry took the map with the activities and said, "You'll see."

Opening the door, fresh air caressed their faces, and birds' chirping echoed. Henry walked out to breakfast. He listened to the sound of leaves in the wind and the river swishing between the trees. *I really needed this,* he thought. He joined his family for breakfast while they planned the day's activities.

"These are the options for today," said Henry, looking at the documents he printed. "Horseback riding, fishing, waterskiing, climbing the mountain, or exploring the forest."

"Why don't we explore the forest while we walk towards the caretakers? On the map, it says they are two miles away," said Susan.

They all agreed.

They finished the fruits and bagels, took some snacks and water, and headed to the forest.

The family followed the map towards the caretakers. Soon, a stream crossed the trail in front of them. The water seemed normal, but on the other side, a cluster of very tall horsetail plants blocked their sight. They walked along the bank and found a path through horsetail.

Henry glanced at the river. The water flowed around stones protruding from the stream. "Okay, let's walk over the rocks."

He set his foot on one stone. Took one step, two steps, three steps, and the stone shifted and slipped into the stream. "Damn it," he said, sprinting towards the other side. His shoes were totally soggy.

Susan and the kids guffawed.

"Ugh!" Henry shook his feet. "C'mon, who's next?"

Maya winced, "I won't cross it."

"Try another rock," Henry said.

Susan approached the river and set her first foot. "I'll go." She took one step, two steps…

"Not that one," Henry said.

Susan moved her foot to the rock besides; it didn't shift, and she managed to cross all the way.

"Way to go, Mom," said Maya. The kids followed her mother's steps.

Henry continued on the trail between the horsetail plants. Not far on the other side, the path ended. A floral and aromatic breeze moved through his nostrils. He closed his eyes, expanded his lungs, and enjoyed the moment. The breeze went away, and he opened his eyes; before him stood trees at least two hundred feet tall, each branch sprouting distinct leaves and colors.

That's new, Henry thought.

They gawked at the surrounding beauty. Everything was so green. The colored birds looked like a watercolor painting.

They walked a minute below the canopy and arrived at a meadow stretched around a large pond. Susan pointed at a small hut beside the pond. "Look, perhaps the caretakers live there?"

As they approached the structure, an old woman came out. She had long white hair and wore scruffy, rustic brown clothes. On her finger was a sparkling crystal ring. Behind her, an elderly person exited the hut too. The person wore a hooded cloak. A long hair was all Henry could see of the person's face.

The woman walked towards Henry, staring, and placed herself inches away from him. She caressed his cheek with tears in her eyes.

What the—? Henry's eyes darted to his family, confused.

The woman approached Moris and Maya and caressed their cheeks too. Susan went and moved her children away from the old woman.

"Hello Susan, Henry, Moris and Maya," the old woman said. "We are the caretakers. Have you found something magical in the forest?" she asked.

"What's your name?" Susan asked.

"I'm Cecilia."

"Well, Cecilia, so far, so good. The cabin is beautiful and the forest incredible."

"Glad to hear," Cecilia said.

"Thank you," said Susan. "Now, can you help us with the activities and its equipment?"

"Of course."

Henry looked at the boat on the dock. "Can we go fishing?"

Horses neighed behind the hut.

"Can we go horseback riding?" asked Moris.

"Yes, I want to ride a horse," said Maya.

"Is it possible?" Susan asked Cecilia.

Cecilia nodded.

"Okay, you go with Mom, and I'll go fishing," Henry told them.

Cecilia and the elder man went inside the hut, and seconds later, they brought all the equipment required.

What the-? Henry pulled a face, mystified that all the equipment was in their small hut.

"We'll help you settle," Cecilia said.

"I'm okay." Henry grabbed his equipment and headed to the boat. The lake glistened light blue, and fishes glowed just beneath the surface. He remembered the dolphins and the sea turtles and shivered about it. He looked back at his family. His mind said *Don't*, but his heart said *Do it*. He went inside the boat with the fishing rod and rowed out.

After several minutes of trying to fish, he had no luck. He moved from place to place, and no fish hooked on his rod.

At three in the afternoon, a thunderstorm formed in the sky.

Henry had the fishing rod in the water when all of a sudden, the water swirled and frothed as it seemed to inhale everything on the surface. It sucked the fishing pole right from Henry's hands. He jerked back, shuddering with horror. Under the water, a green light blinked, each time brighter than the last time. The light hypnotized Henry, and before he knew what he was doing, he dove out of the boat and swam down towards the light.

On the shoreline, Moris's horse took off at a full gallop.

He cried, shuddering, "Mom, help!" He couldn't control the horse and barely held on to the reins as it galloped through the trees. Soon, he fell headfirst into the blackness of a deep pit that was covered in leaves and found himself caught, suspended on tree roots jutting into the hole.

A green light glowed on and off below Moris. Tangled in tree branches, Moris struggled to reach the light. He twisted, stretched his arm, and took the light—at the same time that Henry also grabbed it under the water.

Their bodies straightened, hard, as if they were being stretched by the hands and feet. Their hair stood like a porcupine. They shrieked in agony as their eyes rolled back. Their bodies glowed green in the darkness, and crowd noise sounded loud.

Moris passed out. Henry, barely conscious, was horrified.

Drowning and running out of air, Henry raced for the surface with the green light in his hand.

***

Moris woke up dizzy with blurred vision. "What happened?"

he asked himself.

"Moris? Moris! Are you okay? Answer me," said Susan.

Moris rubbed his head, peered up at the sky outside the pit, and answered weakly, "I think I'm okay."

"Are you sure? Are you bleeding?"

Moris touched his entire body. "I don't think so."

"Okay, let me go for a rope," Susan said. "Maya, stay here with him."

Trapped in the roots, Moris waited for his Mom to return. He twisted around, trying to get comfortable, and in the movement, he saw something below him. He stretched his arm as far as he could and grabbed the thing. The darkness of the pit limited his vision, so he felt it over. Longer than his hand, the object was fairly light but hard and rounded. One end was flat, and the other came to a dull point. He stuffed it in his jacket.

Maya leaned over the edge of the pit. Below, Moris turned over and contorted himself.

She called down, "Are you okay, Moris?"

"Yes. I'm just trying to get out of this. I'm tangled." Moris groaned, struggling, and freed himself. He sighed, and a rope fell from above.

His Mom's head appeared, saying, "Tie it at your hip."

Moris did as asked. "Okay, you can start pulling."

"I can't pull you. You need to climb, and we'll help."

Moris hesitated. "How am I supposed to climb?"

Silence hung for a moment.

"Use the roots. They might support your weight," said Susan.

Moris grabbed some roots and tugged hard. They didn't come off. He began climbing. One step up, two steps, three steps. A root snapped under his foot and in the air. Susan and Maya grasped the rope tight. In a panic, Moris reached out for another root. He froze, startled.

"*Moris*, are you okay?" Susan asked.

Moris panted.

"Moris?"

"Yes, I'm okay."

"Can you keep climbing?"

"I don't want to; I'm scared."

"You need to. And fast, the roots can break off again."

A cracking sound echoed. "Oh, no," quavered Moris. He hurried his climb.

Susan and Maya pulled harder, and Moris managed to get out of the well. Throwing himself on the ground, he panted for seconds.

"Thank god you're okay," said Susan, hugging Moris. She's shaking.

Moris laid still for a while. "I want to go to the cabin."

"Yes, of course." Susan gave a hand to Moris. "Let's return the horses, first."

"And Moris' horse?" asked Maya.

"It ran off. We'll let the caretakers know. Maybe it will return by itself. Come on, let's go," said Susan and headed back to the cabin.

*****

Henry heaved himself back into the boat, panting for air and terrified. He took several long, deep breaths, then looked at the thing in his hands. The horn of some animal, as big as his hand and carved with symbols. He frowned. *Where have I seen this?* He paddled to land, and his family wasn't there, neither the caretakers. So he rushed to search for Susan at the cabin. His hands wringing on the way to the cabin while his heart pounded.

He paced, obsessing about what had just happened under the water. He stared at the horn, trying to come to terms with the situation. *I've seen this before*, he thought again. An image flashed in his mind—the entrance gate.

Something rustled in the forest nearby. He hid the horn in his jacket. After a few moments, his mother, and siblings emerged from the woods. He pretended like nothing happened and tried to remain calm. The last thing he wanted was to worry his mother.

"I have a headache," Moris said.

"Henry, thank god you're here," Susan said, rushing over. "Moris just fell down a pit. It's a miracle he wasn't injured."

Henry did hear her, but his mind wouldn't let go of the horn and the light.

"Henry? Are you even listening to me?" Susan growled.

"No—yes, I–I'm listening," Henry stammered. "Thank god Moris is okay."

Susan looked over at Henry. "Why are you soaking wet?"

"I—I … I accidentally dropped the fishing rod into the water," Henry said. "I dived after it but couldn't find it."

"Well, thank god you are okay too," Susan said. "Let's all

take the afternoon off before lunch. Go wash up, you smell fishy. I'll cook."

Henry struggled with his thoughts. *Should I tell them what happened?* He imagined his mother's overreaction, and that said it all. He remained quiet about his morning and followed the family inside the cabin.

"Are you okay, Moris?" asked Henry as his siblings sat in the living room. "How did the accident happen?"

"I was riding the horse, and out of nowhere, it went insane. I fell off and into a pit. That's the last thing I remember. Then Mom found me."

"Good to know you are okay." He touched Moris's shoulder. "I'm gonna shower."

Henry headed to his room, turned the water on, and left his jacket with the horn over the bed. He entered the shower. Cold water drummed his head; he rubbed his eyes, then stood with one hand on the wall and stared at the floor. *What the hell happened?* He kept musing. After several minutes, he'd gotten nowhere with his thoughts. *I need a drink.*

He finished bathing, walked downstairs, and grabbed a drink. He sat down at the table, staring at the window and squeezing the horn in his pocket.

After a couple of drinks, Henry relaxed. Dinner was ready, and all the family sat down to eat.

Susan had a smile on her face.

"Why are you smiling, Mom?" asked Henry as he bit the meat.

Susan paused, glanced at everyone, and said, "I'm just enjoying being together. Just us, and no distractions." She grabbed her glass and sipped. "Okay, it's time for a joke …

Why did the bike fall over?"

"Mmm, because no one knew how to use it?" said Maya.

Moris said, "No, because there was no stand."

"Ha! No, because it was two tired," Susan said, laughing. No one else laughed.

"I have one," said Moris. "Why did the selfie go to prison?"

"Why?" asked Maya.

"Because it was framed. Hahaha."

In retaliation, Susan didn't laugh.

"Oh, c'mon, Mom. You know you wanted to laugh," said Maya.

Dinner was pleasant, almost like the days when their father was there. By the time they finished, it was ten o'clock.

"Henry, let's play The Game," Moris said. "Yesterday, you promised that we would play, no matter what."

"Yeah, Henry," Maya said. "You promised."

"Shower first," Henry said. "There's one shower for you kids. Who wants to be first?"

Maya said, "Me."

"Be fast; the water heater isn't working."

"Henry, can we start The Game while Maya showers?" Moris asked.

"Sure."

Maya and Susan hurried through their showers. The boys started The Game, their jackets on. Unbeknownst to either, both had their horns in their pockets.

Moris dashed to the bed.

Henry asked, "What world do you wanna travel?"

The bed trembled on its own.

Henry and Moris jerked in surprise. "What was that?" asked Moris.

"I don't know," Henry said. He remembered last night when the headboard had vibrated.

"Let's go to…"

The headboard began to glow brighter and brighter until it made them squint.

"What the hell?" Henry struggled to get out of the bed.

The bedsheet lit up in various colors. The defined images appeared. People and places never seen before by a human emerged; noises and voices echoed louder.

"What's happening?" cried Moris.

The next instant, the bed spun around. They scrambled under the covers as the spinning got faster. Moris's foot smacked Henry in the stomach. Henry's head collided with Moris's forehead. They both bellowed in pain.

"Moris! Try to grab me," said Henry.

Moris's body crashed into Henry's, and they grasped each other.

Soon, a black circle surrounded by blue sparks formed around the bed. The bed fell through the air. Their hearts leaped into their mouths, and their own screams surrounded them—like torture.

The bed fell and fell.

Then it crashed onto the ground.

Both boys dropped off the bed.

Henry lay on the ground, groaning. A high-pitched hissing disturbed his ears. He tried to open his eyes—darkness. He tried again. Nothing. He touched his eyes and

gasped. They were already open.
He was blind.

CHAPTER 4
WHERE ARE WE?

Henry was stunned. He rubbed his ears, trying to clear the hissing sound. He crawled, shuddering in terror, and yelled, "Moris, where are you?"

"Moris?" Henry hollered louder.

The hissing sound faded away, and the noises solidified into explosions.

"I'm here," Moris called back, fear in his voice.

"Don't move. Stay there."

"I can't see. I can't *see*," Moris repeated over and over.

"I'm coming to you. Stay where you are, but keep yelling." Henry kept crawling and calling out for Moris. He felt dirt and grass in his hands. Moments that felt like hours later, Henry touched Moris and then embraced him. "Are you okay?" he asked, stroking Moris's hair and wiping the tears away.

"What happened to us? Where are we? I'm scared—I can't see," Moris gibbered.

"Are you hurt?"

"No, where are we?"

Henry tried to figure it out, but between the pounding heart and the ever-nearing blast noises, he had no idea. "Let's use the bed for cover."

They crawled around to reach out for the bed. They searched and searched as the explosions got louder and closer. His hands couldn't find the bed—only dirt.

"Are we near the bed yet?" Moris asked.

"Moris…" Henry's voice was slow. "I can't see either."

"What the heck? No, no, no. Henry! What are we going to do? You can't see, I can't see. We're going to die here," gibbered Moris. "I don't want to crawl around. We are doomed."

Henry crawled faster, his breath quickened, and his heart raced. He searched for Moris and held him. Both trembled.

All they could do was yell for help.

****

Maya finished her bath and hurried to Henry's room to play The Game. No one was there, and the bed was still made.

"Henry? Moris? Where are you?" Maya glanced around the room. "Are we playing Marco Polo? I say Marco, you say Polo."

No one answered.

"Marco?"

She searched below the bed. She looked behind the dresser. She turned on the closet light. It was empty. Turning to leave, she flicked off the light, and a screech echoed from under the hardwood floor.

"Are you here, Henry?" she whirled back and turned the

lights back on. She glanced at the floor and found a trap door. She knelt down and knocked on the wooden floorboards; it sounded hollow. Maya felt around for a button or trigger to open it. In the closet's corner, she found a book covered in dust. She grabbed it and blew the dust off. It was an antique black rubber notebook with blank pages. She took it and kept searching for her brothers.

"Mom? Have you seen Henry and Moris?"

"They're supposed to be in Henry's room."

"I know, but they aren't there."

"What?" Susan called out in shock. "Henry? Moris? Where are you, boys?"

They searched the entire house.

"Boys?" Susan yelled, the panic rising. "This is no time to play around. Tell us where you are." She went outside. "Henry? Moris? I really need you to show yourself. Stop playing around, please."

The thought petrified Susan that they could disappear like their father.

***

In the darkness, the brothers began to panic. "What are we going to do, Henry? Can you see yet?" asked Moris.

"No."

"Me either. I hear explosions's closer."

"We need to get away from the explosions." Henry pondered. "Do you have a belt?"

"Yes?"

"Give it to me."

Henry took off his belt and linked it with Moris's, "Hold on to the belt."

Moris grasped it while Henry tied it to his wrist. He searched for a long stick, grabbed it, and said, "Follow me."

Henry walked, moving the stick side to side, testing the ground. He led them down a path. It rose steeply until their legs began to ache.

"Let's crawl," said Henry.

"Are you sure we're even heading in the right direction?" asked Moris, panting.

"Of course, I can see very well," Henry replied, joking. This was Henry's first joke after their Dad had disappeared.

Eventually, they came to a step. After that, the ground was flat.

Running steps approached.

"Hello?" Henry asked, shivering.

"*Cuin soju lem?*" mumbled a woman's voice.

Henry and Moris froze. They didn't understand the language, and the footsteps paced around them. They sounded closer and closer, inches away. Henry shifted Moris to stand behind him. A soft breeze hit his face as if someone waved a hand in front of him.

"*Belus Nomlus?*" the woman asked.

Henry frowned and tried to figure out what language she spoke. He said, "English, please."

"*Irrambulus,*" the woman said.

Silence reigned for a moment.

"Are you still there?" asked Henry.

"Who are you?" replied the woman.

"Oh, thank god," said Henry. "My name is Henry Walcar. Can you please help us? We've had an accident and can't see anything."

"Where did you come from? How did you get here?" the woman asked, still pacing around them.

"We don't know. We just crashed here, blinded. Please help us."

Moris clung to Henry's arm. The explosions receded into the distance.

The footsteps stopped, and the woman mumbled something under her breath. "Drink this," she said louder as she put a bottle into Henry's hand. "This healing potion will restore your sight. This is a common thing for outsiders."

"Healing potion? Outsiders?" asked Henry, wondering who she was.

"Drink it, and you'll see." She chortled at her own pun.

Suspicious, Henry opened the bottle and sniffed. It smelled similar to freshwater.

After drinking the potion, the blackness receded from the corners, light slowly seeped back through. Henry's vision returned.

"Be careful; you can get dizzy," the woman said.

Henry recovered his sight and stood up. He handed the drink to Moris, who took a cautious sip, then stood up and hugged Henry. Moris was trembling, and Henry worried the boy was overwhelmed by their experience.

Henry glanced around. Before them were trees; he turned back and saw a hole in the ground. He didn't recognize the landscape.

The young woman before them was shorter than Henry, with dark medium-length hair and striking green eyes. She wore dark pants, a redshirt, and a red hoodless cloak.

"Thank you," Henry said. "What was the liquid we just drank?"

"I told you before, a potion to bring your vision back," she growled. After a pause, she added, "I'm Glinda."

"I'm Henry, and this is my brother, Moris." Henry offered to shake hands, but Glinda left him hanging.

"Now that you've recovered, tell me how you got here," Glinda said, glancing around quickly as if she expected someone. "You're not from around here."

"I was going to ask you the same thing," Henry said. "We don't know how we got here. We're from Texas. You?"

"Texas?" Glinda frowned

"Yes, Texas."

"Still not getting it."

"It's in the United States," Moris said with a mocking voice.

Glinda shrugged. "And why am I supposed to know where this United … thing is?"

The brothers looked at each other, concerned.

Henry frowned, shaken. "Where are we?"

Glinda leaned back, scratched her jaw.

"United States is on Earth, you know?" Moris said.

"Oh! Strakum World?"

Moris's mockery disappeared. The boys stared at each other. "What do you mean 'Strakum World'? Where are we?" Moris asked.

"Strakum World is where humans live," Glinda explained, echoing Moris's mocking tone. "This is Dantus World, in another Universe."

"Dan—What?" Moris stammered.

"*Dantus* World," Glinda repeated, annoyed. "This world differs from Earth. You're in where wizards live. Where magic happens." She shouted the last word, lifting her arms to the sky as if expecting a lightning bolt might strike her.

"Ha! Come on, a wizard?" Henry snorted. "Where are we really? The Amazon? New Zealand?"

"Amazon? Zee-land?" asked Glinda. She stepped back, whirled to the side, and stretched out her arm. An icy breeze started, then blew harder and harder until the brothers were quite cold. The breeze gathered on her palm in mini-tornado. She shouted, "*Ventrulum*!"

A windstorm puffed out from her palm, blowing the branches off the trees and shifting the surrounding rocks and twigs.

Glinda looked smug.

"Wow!" Moris exclaimed. "That's awesome. How did you do that? Do it again, do it again."

Henry furrowed his brow.

"You believe me now? As I said, this world is called Dantus, where all wizards live."

"I'm still confused. How do you know English?" Henry asked.

"I made a spell to learn the languages of our visitors," she said with obvious pride.

"Visitors?" Henry wondered how many had been

through the same terrifying experience.

"You think you're the first to come here? We get people from many Universes: Manjara, Dehity, Klengi, Troby, and others. Although, you are the first humans. We didn't know your kind could travel across worlds. Your turn to answer questions — how did you get here?"

Moris tugged Henry's shirt for him to bend over and whispered, "Is this real?"

Glinda stepped closer. "Humans? How did you get here?"

Before Henry could speak, a tremendous blast shook the forest. The brothers cringed, but Glinda ignored it. On the horizon, Henry could see flashes of colored light with each bang.

"What was that?" asked Moris after a red explosion.

Henry was convinced they had indeed landed in another Universe. He had no idea how they were going to get back.

Glinda didn't answer. She was too focused on the coming battle. The explosions were still getting closer.

"Who are they?" asked Henry.

"The girl with the red cloak, like me, is Tallye, and the boy is Galio, my best friend," Glinda said. "We are called Veneficums. The old man with the blue cloak is Bastian, and the girl Nabí; they're Milaculums. Be careful with them."

The battle approached as the Milaculums chased the Veneficums toward their position. Henry wanted to run and hide, but nothing seemed safe enough.

The wizards all paused, noticing the humans in their midst. Henry watched the previously smug Glinda wring her hands.

On the side of Henry and Moris were Glinda, Tallye, and Galio. Yards before them were the two blue-cloaked Milaculums.

One of them, Bastian, had the symbol they'd seen at the forest gate on his cloak.

Bastian scowled. "These people are not from here. Who are they?"

"They're from the Strakum World, and one is just a child."

Bastian's face fell when he heard they were humans. Without warning, he snapped his fingers and tossed a bolt of lightning toward the brothers, shattering the glass potion bottles they still held. Henry and Moris both flinched, but when Moris moved, his horn fell out of its jacket pocket to the ground.

Bastian's eyes twitched when he saw the horn. "*Irrambulus*," he cursed, aghast. He teleported to grab the horn, but Tallye anticipated his movement and built a defensive shield to protect them.

"Destroy the shield," Bastian shrieked at Nabí.

Bastian flung out his arm, casting a spell. An intense electricity gathered in the air, prickling Henry's skin. He watched, both frightened and fascinated, as blue sparkles formed at Bastian's palms. With a great, crackling thrust, the wizard unleashed a stream of lightning at the shield.

Nabí joined with her own lightning stream. The brothers inside the shield hunkered down, petrified.

"You can't hurt us," Tallye said, her voice shaky. "Sister, leave now with Bastian before the others arrive."

Henry frowned. *Sister?*

Bastian muttered another spell. An aura appeared around him, and his energy increased. With one hand, he kept striking with lightning, and with the other, he closed his hand into a fist and shrank the shield.

It shocked Henry and Moris. They tried to run away, but Glinda grabbed them.

"You're safer with me," she said.

The shield cracked, and Tallye's smile faded. It couldn't block Bastian's attack for much longer.

The crack got larger. Glinda and Galio stood ready to fight.

Tallye said, "Get the humans and the horn out of here," she said to Glinda. "We can't let them take the horn."

Moris bent and snatched it off the ground. He shoved it back into his jacket pocket.

"Go to the castle," Tallye ordered. "We'll hold Bastian and Nabí. Run."

Glinda dragged the brothers away. "We need to go," she yelled, desperate.

Glinda took out a potion and gave it to the brothers. "Drink this; you'll need it." Henry and Moris really had no choice this time. They drank the liquids down and raced off.

Henry felt he was running normally, but when he looked at his legs, they were pumping much faster than he expected. Even his reflexes were enhanced; he dodged holes and fallen trees with ease.

They passed lakes under enormous colored rocky mountains, their shapes looming like the ones near the forest. Seconds later, a round, hairy animal with wings flew beside Moris. It had long ears and small legs.

"Henry? Are you seeing this?" Moris asked.

Not much later, they arrived at a castle gate. It was almost the same gate symbol as at the cabin, only here both horns pointed down.

Glinda ended up panting and cursing as she paced back and forth. She then headed to a fountain behind her and washed her face.

"That was amazing!" Moris said. "Did you see the flying animals and the white mountains?"

"I saw the mountains, and not only the white ones, also the green, orange, and red ones."

Moris whispered, "What are we gonna do, Henry?"

"We have to get home," Henry said. "Keep your horn to yourself; it obviously causes a lot of trouble. Where did you find that, anyway?"

Moris explained what happened in the pit. When he was finished, Henry confessed to Moris about his horn and what happened in the fishing boat. As he finished, Glinda approached them.

Henry hissed to Moris, "Don't tell them I have one."

"What's with all the flying pigs?" Moris asked.

Glinda smirked. "You humans know nothing about the Universes. What you called a flying pig we call a Bolly. Now, how the heck did you get that horn, kid?"

Moris hesitated and glanced at Henry for guidance.

Henry said, "I bought it for him as a souvenir, back in our world. Why do you ask?"

Glinda shrugged. "No reason. Let's go inside."

Entering the gate, the brothers gaped. Before them loomed a huge castle, built with enormous grey stones and topped with a dark roof. Statues of men and women with wings ringed the structure as if guarding it. The main door stood sixty feet tall, the ancient wood carved with different symbols and maps.

Henry looked around, wide-eyed. "This is really something."

They entered a big room. In the middle of it was a round table. Above, a very large ceiling lamp. Along one wall, wood stairs led up to the rest of the castle.

"This is the Gonlu Room," said Glinda.

They walked below the ceiling light, and suddenly, the chandelier scrambled. Moris grabbed Henry in horror.

"Ha! Humans," giggled Glinda.

At the end of the Gonlu Room was a long hallway, and at the other end, they found the inner courtyard. It was crowded by other wizards like Glinda, all practicing spells and their magic.

Glinda led the brothers across the yard, threading between the Veneficums. As they moved, Henry felt heat on his neck. He glanced around and saw a child wizard making fire appear in the air near him.

"Awesome!" Moris said.

Henry watched a wizard with sparks in his hand and thrust it into another wizard's cloak. The cloak caught fire, and the other wizard jerked to put it out. Henry frowned, then paid closer attention to their cloaks. One of them had a very similar symbol as Bastian; only the horns were pointed differently.

The wizards were practicing spells and magic. Others were playing and eating. It reminded Henry of his summer camps when he was a kid—one full of kids *pretending* to be wizards. This one was full of actual, real wizards.

Henry watched his brother gape at the wizards. "You're enjoying this, right?"

"You bet I am. This is what I always dreamed of."

"We need to be careful."

Moris was looking around when he stumbled over a Veneficum. The wizard ignored him and kept walking. Moris turned to say sorry, but fell silent; the wizard's cloak had only a half-symbol. Only one horn on it?

A few Veneficums had a half-symbol. Most of them had no symbol at all, like Glinda. What did it mean? Full-symbol? Half-symbol? No symbol at all?

Moris nudged Henry in the ribs. "Look at their cloaks."

"I know; the Milaculum had the same symbol as the forest gate. These wizards have the symbol of the castle's gate."

They kept following Glinda.

Glinda said, "Let me take you to Lucio. Lucio is one of the oldest wizards. He'll be interested in talking to you." She let them down another hallway.

Henry wondered if Lucio had met any humans before. "How much does he know about us?" he asked.

"The eldest Veneficums are Lucio and Iggy. They know so much about the Universes, but I don't know what they know about Strakum. We've never received a human. So here we are; this is Lucio's private study."

Inside, a wizard perched on a tall chair behind a desk. Both were made from the same wood as the cabin's magical headboard. The wizard himself wore a red cloak and a scowl. He had short-dark hair, brown eyes, and wrinkles on his forehead. On the stone wall behind him, hung a portrait of an endless dark room.

"Lucio, we found these humans close to the battlefield," said Glinda. Her earlier sarcasm had disappeared.

Lucio pulled a face. "You said 'humans'?" He then paused. "Where is Tallye?"

Glinda hesitated. "She stalled Bastian so we could escape. The child has a horn." Glinda clasped her hands together to stop the shuddering.

Lucio scratched his jaw. "A horn?" In a delicate manner, he got up from the chair. His cloak had the full symbol on it.

Lucio approached Moris. "What's your name, kid?"

"I'm Moris, and we are humans, we're from … Strakum World. I think that's what you call it."

"Ha! Where did you get the horn?"

Henry said, "I'm Henry, and this is my little brother. I gave the horn to him as a present, back on Earth."

"Can I see it?"

Moris hesitated, not knowing what to do. Henry nodded.

Moris took out his horn and handed it over to Lucio.

Lucio grabbed the horn and squinted at it. The horn turned dark red at his touch. Seconds later, Lucio's skin melted off. "Wow, that's hot." He tossed the horn back to Moris, who caught it with no problem.

"Why did it burn your hand?" asked Henry.

"I'm not sure," Lucio said. He gazed at Moris. "And I don't know how you can hold it either."

Henry decided it would be best to continue hiding his own horn.

"They must be tired," Lucio said to Glinda. "Take them to a pleasant room where they can sleep well. And don't forget to give them the potion for the blindness."

Henry pursed his brow. *Are we going to need regular doses?*

After leaving Lucio's den, Tallye found them. She was alone, panting, and her face covered with dirt and scratches.

"Tallye, are you okay? What happened? Where is Galio?" asked Glinda.

"We lost Galio!" Tallye cried.

"Lost as in dead? Or they took him away?"

"It was awful. Bastian struck us hard. We couldn't match Bastian's force. Galio sacrificed himself to save me," Tallye said.

"No," Glinda cried.

Tallye passed beside the humans and walked away. Henry and Moris hadn't realized until now that Tallye had half of the symbol on her cloak—the round figure and within, one horn, one wristband, and the spear.

Ahead of them, Glinda walked with slumped shoulders.

Moris whispered to Henry, "Should we ask her what the symbol means?"

Henry glared at Moris and shook his head.

"Glinda, what do the symbols mean?" Moris asked anyway.

Henry groaned.

"The less you know, the better for you."

Henry turned to his brother and grasped his arm. "You need to do what I tell you. We don't know these people—wizards—whatever they are."

Moris snorted. There was an awkward silence while they followed Glinda to their room.

They approached a flight of stairs, but not any ordinary ones. The wooden treads creaked with every step. Hung on the stone walls were portraits of many generations of wizards, along with pictures of angels and supernatural-looking tigers with big teeth and owls with enormous claws.

Their little group reached a long hallway with many doors for bedrooms. As they passed, Henry glanced inside the few open doors. In one, there was a wizard hovering over cards; next, a girl was sparking fire on her fingers. The following, a wizard was pouring water into a glass. Another, a girl was blowing her hair dry without a hair blower.

"This is your room," Glinda said, pausing in front of an empty room. "Get some rest. Tomorrow morning we can talk more about your arrival."

Glinda started to leave, then turned back around.

"Oh, I almost forgot. Here is the potion. You need to sip some of it tonight before sleep and again in the morning. If you don't drink it—well, you know." She magically made two glass bottles of a dark red potion out of the air, which then transformed into crystal water.

"Understood," Henry said. "Thank you. And goodnight."

The room was small and gloomy, with two single beds, a

table between them, and two small armoires. On the back wall, a window overlooked the courtyard and the castle's outskirts.

Henry opened the armoire. It smelled old and woody. "They forgot to give us clothes," he said.

After those words, pajamas magically appeared on a hanger. "Moris, you need to see this," he said, excited.

Moris opened his armoire, and his sleepwear appeared hanging. "This is so cool."

Moris bounced on the bed. "Can you believe where we are? We are in the wizard's world!" His voice became a nearly shriek. "I told you I can make things happen."

Henry winced at the volume. "This is crazy."

"Are we going home right away?"

"Mom and Maya must be worried sick."

"Maya would finally believe in magic. We are in the Dantus' World," Moris said, still enthusiastic.

"Stop! It's dangerous here. Galio died for us, don't you understand? This world has terrible people with strong powers. We're just humans. We must go back."

Moris's energy dissipated. "I know. You're right."

"Did you see Lucio's chair?"

"What about it?"

"It looked very similar to the headboard. Maybe they know something about the bed that brought us here. I'll ask tomorrow morning. But Moris, I'll do the talking. You stay quiet … Drink your potion."

"Okay." He glanced out the window. Their room was situated almost at the very top of the castle. "Henry? Look."

Outside, stars wheeled across the dark blue sky. Two moons also lit the night, one orange and the other light red. On the ground, birds glowed in the dark, the same as the deer and other animals.

"Wow, that's so incredible," Henry said.

"You know, today was the most amazing, confusing, and scary thing … Dad would love it." Tears began trickling down Moris' cheek, and he turned to hide them. "Love you, Henry. Goodnight." He slipped under the bedsheets.

Henry forced his own tears back. In his own shaky voice, he said, "Me too, little bro. Thank god we are okay."

He crawled into his own bed and shut his eyes. After an extraordinary day, sleep came quickly.

CHAPTER 5
THE MYSTERIOUS LAND

It was long after dark, and Susan searched the cabin for her children. "Henry? Moris?" she called.

She then went outside to the trees around the dwelling. "Boys? … Boys!" Her breathing got faster.

Her eyes darted around as she searched for the boys. Heart racing as sweat dripped down her forehead. Her entire world was falling apart. *This can't be happening. This can't be happening;* she kept the mantra while fear invaded her. Thoughts of never seeing her sons again swirled in her head.

She rushed inside, "Maya? Where are you?"

"I'm here, Mom." Maya came running downstairs, gasping and wailing.

Susan went to her and kneeled, her hands trembling as she held Maya's arms. "Stay with me; I don't want you to lose you too. Do you understand?"

"Yes, Mom," Maya cried, wiping her face. She fumbled the notebook she'd grabbed from upstairs and a photograph slipped out.

Susan picked up the picture. "What's this?"

"I don't know. I found it in Henry's room."

Susan peered at the picture, astonished. She asked, "Is this the old lady, the caretaker?"

In the photograph were four youngsters, two boys, and two girls. One of the women looked like the caretaker but much younger.

"I think so," Maya said.

"The caretakers! Let's go." Susan searched for a flashlight and found it in a drawer.

They hurried through the woods by the light of the full moon. Howling echoed through the trees, birds flew from their nests, deer, and horses ran and galloped—it seemed something also disturbed all the animals tonight. Susan grasped Maya, scared, and hastened to the caretakers.

Arriving at the darkened hut, knocked on the door, shouting the woman's name. "Cecilia? Cecilia?" No one answered. She went to a window, shone her flashlight through it, and looked inside. The hut was empty.

"What's going on, Mom?"

Susan hesitated. "We need to get a phone signal and call the police."

They hurried back to their cabin. The animals were in a frenzy. Something definitely was coming, and the howling grew louder and pitching.

Back at their own cabin, Susan grabbed the car keys. They sprinted to the car and drove all the way back to the highway in search of a phone signal. As they passed the forest gate, a dazzling white-pink light illuminated the forest behind them.

"What's happening?" Maya asked, quavering.

"No idea, but we need to call the police."

Along the dirt road, they passed the mountains, the bizarre weather, and soon they were on the highway with the billboard, *Coffee Cheer, Morning Cheers.*

Susan made the call. It took thirty minutes for the officers to arrive, and Susan rushed to explain her missing sons while Maya waited in the car.

One officer said, "Where did you say is this entrance to the cabin?"

"Over there," Susan pointed towards the dirt road.

There was no dirt road, only bushes.

"What the—?" Susan's eyes widened.

"Ma'am, there's nothing there," said the officer.

Susan, stunned, walked to the bushes. A shiver ran down her spine. "It was here. The road was here; we just drove on it."

"Ma'am, we don't see a road. Are you sure this is where you were?"

"Yes, I'm sure. It was next to this sign."

The officer frowned. "Are you feeling okay, ma'am?"

Susan growled, "No, I'm not. My sons are missing."

"I heard you before, but where did they go missing?"

"In the cabin, and the road was right here." She gestured to the bushes and paced side to side. Her eyes twitched.

"You need to calm down, ma'am. We want to help, but we don't see a road."

Susan said nothing and headed through the bushes, searching for a road. Maya got out of the car and followed.

"What are you doing, ma'am?" asked the officer. "There's nothing over there, you're just going to get bitten by a snake. Come, let me take you home."

Susan found nothing. Suddenly, her chest became so tight that it was near impossible to breathe. The pain fisted around her heart, expanding in her ribs until her knees went weak. She knelt to the ground, gasping for air before the pain overwhelmed her, and she collapsed.

"Mom!" yelped Maya. "Officers, help!"

The officers rushed to Susan and checked her pulse. "She's breathing, but we need to go right now." They picked her up and put her inside the cop car.

Maya sat beside her. The siren wailed in Maya's ear, the flashing lights blurred the outside world. Maya sobbed, embracing her mother, scared to get close to her heart and not hear it beat.

They arrived at the ER, and the doctors took Susan inside.

"Should we call your father?" One of the doctors asked Maya.

She shook her head, wailing. "We are alone."

***

Susan opened her eyes slowly. Her sight was blurry, and her body too weak to move. "Maya, are you here?"

Maya gasped, "Mom." She rushed over and hugged her.

Susan looked around as the blur faded away. "Where am I?" she asked.

"At the hospital. You fainted. They said you almost had

a heart attack."

Susan groaned. "I feel so weak. How long have I been here?"

"Just a couple of hours … Nurse," called Maya.

The nurse came in. "Oh good, you're awake. Take it slow; let me call the doctor."

As the nurse retreated, the police entered.

"Officer, did you find my sons?"

"No, ma'am. We've been with you."

"I don't want to lose you too, Mom," Maya said, holding Susan's hand.

"Do you have a photo of the boys?"

Susan asked Maya for her purse and handed over a picture. The officer copied down all the information. He finished, gave his phone number, and left.

"Maya?" Groaned Susan as she leaned forward. "Help me get up."

"You need to rest, Mom."

"We need to get back to the cabin." Susan sat on the edge of the bed. Maya gave her shoulder, and Susan leaned against her and got up.

"Wow, wow, what are you doing?" said the doctor as he entered.

"I'm feeling okay. We need to leave."

"You need to rest." The doctor approached Susan and tried to sit her down.

"No." She shooed off the doctor's arm. "I'm not sick. I can rest at home."

The doctor sighed. "As you wish."

Susan walked out with her daughter and called for a taxi.

It was sunrise.

When the taxi arrived, she gave directions to the billboard, where her car was. Her eyes closed. She still was weak.

"Mom, we are here."

They got out, and the taxi left. Susan hesitated, trying to process what had happened. She went to look at the bushes again.

"I have no idea what to do, Maya." Hopeless tears fell. "Let's go home and rest. We need to think."

They got in their car, and there was the map Henry had printed. The cabin was gone, no directions shown. "Oh my god! This is crazy. The cabin was right here. How did it disappear?"

The silence in the car said it all.

When they arrived home, Susan called the officer's number. "Officer, this is Susan Walcar, the one with the missing sons…"

"Yes, Ma'am … We are sending a helicopter search and rescue team to the area where we found you. Get some rest, and we'll call you if anything shows up."

"Thank you very much, officer." She hung up.

"Mom, we can't lose them too. First Dad, now them." Maya sobbed.

No words came out of Susan, and she hugged Maya tight. "Why don't you sleep in my bed? I don't want you to be alone."

They went to bed and slept or tried to.

***

In the afternoon, the doorbell sounded. Susan's eyes were

red and wet from crying. She got up, cleaned her tears, and opened the door.

"Robert?" she asked, confused.

"Susan, are you okay?" Robert hugged her.

Susan frowned, not hugging back. "What are you doing here?"

"It's all over the news," he said.

She grimaced and said, "My boys, they disappeared. Out of nowhere. We were on vacation, and they just … vanished. Like Kevin."

Robert twitched at the last words. He said, "I'm really sorry." He caressed her shoulder. "I don't know what to say. How can I help?"

Susan shrugged.

"How did it happen? Tell me," he asked.

Susan invited him in and explained, or tried to because she couldn't understand how it had happened. She told him about the map, the cabin, and how it also disappeared before the police could arrive. She expected judgment or a reaction from Robert, but he said nothing, and his face stood still. She couldn't read him.

"You think I'm crazy, right?"

"No, no. Of course not."

Footsteps echoed from the stairs. Maya said, "She is telling the truth."

Robert nodded. "I believe you."

Susan wasn't sure if he said that to be comforting or he really did believe her.

"Take me to where the road was," said Robert.

Even though Susan didn't think Robert had anything to do with her husband Kevin's disappearance, she hadn't forgotten Henry's theory. Still, she needed all the help she could get. The three of them jumped in the car, and Susan drove out to the billboard.

"Here," said Susan. "The road was right here past the sign. And it showed up on this map."

Robert looked at the map, then went and stared at the bushes. "I don't see a road. Are you sure it was here?"

"I knew you'd think I'm crazy."

"I'm not saying that." Robert went through the bushes and glanced down. "Come, look at this."

"What is it?" Susan asked.

"There are tire marks under the bushes. Somehow a car passed here recently without damaging the bushes."

He found that awfully fast, thought Susan. Yet, it was true. She wondered whether those were her own car's tire marks.

She followed the prints towards the hill, but then they suddenly vanished. Susan was sure they'd driven between those hills.

"What do you want to do?" asked Robert.

"I'll ask the police if they found something on the other side of the hill. Take us home. It's no use for us to be here. There's nothing."

Susan went back to the car. Robert stayed for a while, looking around, then headed back to the car.

Back at the house, Robert dropped the women off. He didn't step out but rolled down the window. "Susan, I need to get back to Vultock. If you need anything, please let me know."

"Thanks, Robert."

Susan entered the house, thinking about Robert's actions. *That's bizarre.*

She turned on the TV, looking for news about her missing sons. She changed to another news channel. Nothing. Another channel; nothing. A harsh gasp ensued. *There's nothing on the news. How did he know?* She turned off the TV and paused for a moment.

She picked up the phone and called the policeman. "Officer, any news? Did you find something on the other side of the hill?"

"No, ma'am. The helicopter hasn't seen any forest or cabin in the area. Are you completely sure your sons went missing around there?"

"Yes…" Susan repeated the story. Now the officer sounded skeptical. She had to find proof.

Susan went to her daughter. "Maya, did you find anything else in the notebook?"

"No. It's blank. No writing, nothing. It only had the photo."

Susan took the diary and examined it herself. The cover of the old leather journal felt rough in her hands. The inside was indeed blank, as a document it had. The last page had a signature that read *Zadkiel Woldie.*

Susan grimaced. "That's weird. Who has a blank diary and puts his signature at the end?"

Susan looked again at the photo. *Cecilia knew something. Where was she? Who are the other three? Who was Zadkiel Woldie?*

On the back of the photo, someone had written, *My loving children.*

"Maya, can you google this man Zadkiel Woldie?"

Maya took out her phone and searched for him. Zero results on the web.

"Damn it."

CHAPTER 6
THE WOOLY ROOM

In the castle, Moris woke first. Back home, Henry hated if anyone woke him up. So Moris stayed put. He peeked around the room, saw the potion that Glinda had given them, and sipped some of it.

He crept to the window and lifted the curtains just a little. A forest stretched out beneath him, the trees twice the size of those on Earth. There was also a lake near the castle that he didn't remember from their dash to safety yesterday. In it, dolphins jumped playfully. *Weird*, he mused. *Dolphins lived only in the sea, didn't they?*

Moris pressed his forehead to the glass. On the grass, the Veneficums seated, legs crossed in meditation. One wizard with no cloak approached a Veneficum and held his hand above the Veneficum's head; seconds later, a light came out of his hands, and the Veneficum's body trembled as he shrieked, excited. The wizard did the same routine to the other Veneficums.

Outside the castle walls, a wizard stood, looking towards Moris's window. Moris gazed back at him. The wizard wore a coat, covering his cloak.

The wizard gestured toward Moris. He started to whirl his arms, and small sparks formed at his fingertips. The potion bottles trembled. Moris jerked in surprise, confused at what had just happened. When Moris looked back at the wizard, he'd vanished.

He waited and waited for Henry to wake up. In a rush of impatience and mounting despair that Henry didn't wake up, he decided to go out exploring. He opened the armoire, and Earth clothes sat there. After dressing, he gently opened the door and peered out. The hallway was clear. He grabbed his jacket, the horn and left the room quietly.

Sneaking down two floors, he peered down a hallway and found a door ajar. He looked both ways before entering. No one was watching. As he entered, he passed through a haze that sent a chill up his spine.

Before him was a gloomy room filled with books. A library.

Despite feeling uneasy, he didn't turn back. From the ceiling hung chandeliers with candles as figures; the wall had marks, paintings of some kind of seahorse with wings and wizards. Each painting he walked past depicted a piece of history. The bookshelves were ordered according to animal figures, and the books had symbols on them.

He approached a bookshelf in the section of a tiger-figure. Dust billowed as he took out a book. He had to be careful, the pages were fragile. In the gloomy room, he opened the book, and suddenly a candle hovered above him.

Moris looked up. "Thanks," he said to the candle.

The book contained spells, figures, drawings and

symbols. He didn't understand any of it and put it back on the shelf.

He passed several bookshelves, and on the third one, a white pedestal stood out in the dark, holding something. On closer examination, he saw a crystal case enclosing an ancient wooden box in the shape of a book.

As he approached the wooden box, his jacket pocket glowed green. With each step closer, the light blinked on and off, faster and faster, as if the horn were about to come alive.

Moris gaped. *I shouldn't be doing this alone,* he thought. He remembered that with Lucio his horn had glowed dark red.

"This isn't my horn," Moris said. It bore different symbols. He had to have grabbed Henry's horn instead.

He was inches from the ancient wooden box when the crystal case opened up on its own.

Moris reached out his arm, and the wooden box trembled. He twitched and yanked his hand back. The book's cover had a round stone figure containing a sword, spear, two horns, and two gauntlet wristbands. If Moris had doubts about the importance of the forest symbol, it was now answered.

The lump in his stomach said something peculiar was in the wooden box. He opened it to find an antique book with the same symbols. The book looked important—well, obviously, it was standing alone on a pedestal.

He took the book carefully, opened it, and dust billowed in the form of symbols. Moris blew it away. He leafed through the first pages and frowned; they were blank. He continued browsing, and in the middle of the book was a page with seven crystal rings. Moris peered at them for a moment and flipped the page.

His eyes widened. On the page were horns just like his and Henry's, with a drawing of a crystal sword, a strange stone, a crystal spear, and two gauntlet wristbands. He didn't hesitate and ripped out the page and hid it in his pocket. Maybe this would help them discover the truth about the horns.

The thought of Henry waking up alone interrupted Moris. He knew Henry would be mad without him in the room. He left so fast he forgot to put the book back inside the wooden box and the crystal case.

He searched for the library's exit but couldn't find it. His heart began to pound as he ran through the bookshelves. Finally, he saw the door and dashed towards it, but out of nowhere, a bolt of energy struck Moris and threw him to the floor. Pulse racing, he stood up and twisted around for the source. A hidden door had appeared in the wall. The horn in his hand beamed green now. Moris approached cautiously. As he was about to open it, he heard a shriek from behind the door.

A normal kid would start running—and Moris too. He dashed away.

He then heard someone entering the library. He immediately hid between the bookshelves, shivering. The steps grow closer and closer. A bead of sweat dribbled down his neck.

A Veneficum went around the bookshelves. Moris

watched, trying not to be heard or seen. His hands were shaking. The Veneficum grabbed a book and started to read. Moris spotted an opportunity to slip out into the hallway.

Just when he closed the door, Glinda came around the corner.

"Kid? What are you doing here? Where is your brother?"

"I–I," Moris stammered. "I wanted to go to the bathroom, but I couldn't find it. Can you take me to it?"

Glinda led Moris to a bathroom and waited for him to finish.

"Let's go get your brother," said Glinda.

As they headed back toward the room, shouting rang out.

It was Henry.

He was howling at another Veneficum, asking about Moris. The Veneficum was babbling, clueless about this strange human yelling at him. Then Henry saw Moris and, running to him, snapped, "What the hell, Moris? Where have you been? You can't leave my sight. This is not a place to be alone with strangers."

"Sorry, Henry," said Moris. "I was looking for the bathroom and you were sleeping; I couldn't hold it. It won't happen again."

"Damn it," Henry paused to relax. "Forgive me for yelling at you. It's just that I'm worried." He hugged Moris. "Let's find out how to get home to Mom and Maya."

"Relax, human. You may be strangers to us, but we don't take you as a threat," Glinda said. "Well … for now. Let's have breakfast with Lucio so we can talk. Have you drunk your potion?"

"Almost forgot," Henry said. He went back for the potion and took a sip.

When they arrived at the Gonlu Room, two Veneficums were hovering and hanging an old portrait of a wizard with a dark red cloak. He had a tetchy face, semi-long hair, his forehead wrinkled, and his eyes squinted.

As the brothers crossed the room, the painting's eyes followed them. He turned to the portrait and suddenly, it winked at him.

"Did you see that?" asked Moris, astonished.

"See what?" asked Glinda

"The painting, it winked at me." Moris wondered how such an image could be so foreboding.

"Actually, this painting is the only picture that hasn't ever moved. Come on, let's go."

"You're right, Moris," Henry said. "His eyes followed me as I walked." He moved forward and backward, testing the portrait.

"You see, and it did wink at me," said Moris.

"Maybe it's a side effect of the potion," said Glinda. "Let's go, humans."

"Wait, who is he?" Henry asked.

"His name is Ivar—or was. Legend says he was the son of the founder of all the wizards. He had a sister named Miranda, and a brother called Remiel. Ivar was the greatest of all of us."

"How did he die?" Moris asked.

"Die? Hmm. We don't know for sure he's dead at all. Some say his brother locked him up forever in a place nobody knows. Others say he died in the New Beginning Battle."

"The New Beginning Battle?" Henry asked.

"You ask too many questions, human. It was the first war between the wizards. Now, stop. We do the interrogations, not you. Let's have breakfast. Lucio is waiting."

They entered the dining hall, and there was Tallye, along with Lucio with his grumpy face.

"Come and join us," Lucio said. "We have a lot to talk about."

Henry and Moris sat down. "Thanks, Lucio," said Henry. "We want to go back home. Do you know how we can get there?"

Lucio said, "Yeah, sure—but you need to tell me first how you got here."

Henry hesitated, then explained how the boys had played The Game. Tallye listened carefully while Lucio looked confused.

"I almost forgot," Henry added. "There was a symbol on the forest's gate that looked very similar to this castle's gate. It had one horn pointing down and the other one up."

Lucio reached inside his robe and pulled out a book. He opened it and showed a figure to Henry. "Is this the symbol you saw?"

"Yes."

Lucio cleared his throat. "Let me get this right. You saw this symbol, at what you called a 'forest' gate', in your world—which looks like our entrance, but instead of a castle inside, it's a cabin?"

Henry said, "That's about right. Why? What does the emblem mean?"

Lucio ignored the question and hissed, "Keep talking."

"That's it, you know the rest. We arrived and Glinda found us."

Henry fell silent as breakfast appeared. Henry and Moris recoiled—they were served dirt wrapped in the wings of an eagle and a black liquid to drink.

"I can't eat this," Moris growled.

Lucio grunted. "Humans! Do you know soil has all the nutrition your body needs?"

"Maybe *your* body," Henry said.

"What do you eat then?"

"Fruits, eggs, and orange juice," said Henry.

Lucio mused. "I have no idea what that means. This spell will turn your plate into whatever food you are thinking of." Lucio hovered his hand above their plate, and with some magic powers, he changed the food into what Henry had asked for.

Lucio frowned.

Henry said, "I would've thought you'd know a lot about us."

"Humans are the least of our concerns," Lucio said. "Except now you have a horn."

"Least of your concerns?"

"Your Universe is the most isolated because it is the youngest of all."

"The youngest? Our Universe is millions of years old."

"Your Universe is like a newborn human baby; ours is

more like in the mid-thirties."

"How many Universes exist?" Henry asked.

"You really are ignorant. There are lots of Universes. Strakum is your Universe where humans live, Dantus is ours; Klengi is where Warkrus live, Manjara where the Manzokans live, Nafty where the Nayiris live. The oldest Universes are the Dehity, where Angels and Demons live, and Troby, where Ratkuls live."

The brothers gawked, taken aback. "Do they all look the same as us?"

"No. Warkrus, Wizards, and you humans too, have similar appearances. The rest look different. Well, maybe the people from Dehity look similar. There are two kinds in Dehity Universe; one looks like us, the other one not." Lucio continued, "We know of your existence. But you humans are powerless and are no threat to our mission. And there is something else about your Universe; it's almost impossible to travel there. That's why I asked how you arrived."

The brother's eyes widened.

"Tallye? After they eat breakfast, show them the library and take them for a walk," Lucio said. "And Glinda, you come with me. We need to talk."

After Glinda had left with Lucio, Henry asked Tallye, "Are you okay after yesterday's fight?"

"I don't want to talk about it," Tallye said, her voice low.

They finished breakfast and went on a tour around the castle. The first stop was the same library Moris had visited that morning. He mentioned nothing.

Moris shuddered. He'd forgotten to replace the book as

it was before. He feared Tallye would find out someone had ripped out a page and know who'd done it.

Henry could see Moris's frightened face. He raised an eyebrow, silently asking Moris what was going on. Moris shook his head.

"The Wooly Room is our library, where you can find the history of the wizards and the Universes," Tallye explained. "There are countless books here; they go back millions of years, and our ancestors left their notes in these books. They contain symbols, spells, stories, legends and much valuable knowledge."

Moris's heart pounded as Tallye got closer to the bookshelf with the pedestal and the antique wooden box. He peered through the bookshelf and discovered the antique book was as he'd found it—inside the box and the crystal case. Someone else must have put it back.

Tallye approached the pedestal, and Moris fidgeted nervously. He peeked at his horn and pushed it further into his pocket, not wanting them to see it glowing. He still had Henry's horn.

"What's in there?" Henry asked Tallye.

"We don't know. This crystal has never been opened. Not even Iggy, the strongest of us, can break it."

Moris was stunned. *Who put the book back inside the crystal?* His mind scrambled to puzzle out the mystery of the crystal and the hidden door. Was he the only one who could open the book?

"How come?" Henry asked.

"I don't know. It's been locked in this crystal since we found it. Similar to the Mortus Door over there." Tallye pointed to the hidden door where Moris had heard the screams. "No one who goes through the door has ever told the story."

"Why not?"

Tallye smirked. "Because no one has ever returned. I wish you well if you enter." She laughed wickedly.

They headed towards the Mortus Door, but Moris hung back and pretended to look at the books. Tallye approached the door, and Moris began to sweat profusely. Tallye opened the door.

"Do you want to go in?"

No one answered. Tallye chuckled. "Let's keep going."

Moris sighed in relief.

Arriving at the front yard of the castle, a Veneficum floated as he exhaled forcefully from his nose. Moris tried the same, and snot came out. Another Veneficum opened his palms and unveiled knives in the air. He turned towards the boys and thrust the knives towards the brothers but then stopped them before their eyes. Henry and Moris halted, shuddering. The knives vanished into dust and the wizard guffawed.

"What the heck, man," howled Henry.

"Hey, Humans? Keep walking," said Tallye.

Later, one wizard created a bubble, trapped another inside it, and moved it sideways. "What the hell? Let me out," the trapped wizard yelled while the others guffawed.

It's like a training camp. They used instruments such as claws, tusks, and spears to practice spells. And besides the wizards, the boys saw animals.

"What are those called?" asked Moris.

Tallye gestured toward a tiger-like animal. "Those are Onakulas, but you can call them tigers, and those are Bukas." She pointed to an owl-like creature.

Tallye left them to talk to another wizard, and Moris took the opportunity to speak freely to his brother. "Henry, I need to tell you something. This morning when you were looking for me, I was in the library."

"What?" Henry said hotly. "You told me you were in the bathroom."

"Listen," Moris replied grimly. "Weird things happened. I woke up before you, and I saw a wizard outside the walls like he was watching us."

"Well, we're the outsiders. They're curious."

"I got a bad feeling about that. He didn't seem to be with these wizards because he had a coat covering his cloak."

Henry snorted. "He could be any wizard walking around the castle."

"Maybe. After that, I went outside the room to kill time, and when I entered the library, I felt a strange tingle." Moris looked down. "The weird thing was when I was approaching the wooden box inside the crystal, your horn glowed green."

"My horn?" Henry asked, confused.

"Yes, I think I grabbed your horn by mistake. Mine has different symbols on it, and this one glowed green. Mine glowed dark red when Lucio grabbed it."

Henry frowned. "Then what happened?"

"Well, when I got closer to the box, the crystal case opened itself."

"What? Tallye said no one has opened it."

"I know, but it opened. There was a book, and on the cover was the forest gate symbol."

Moris pulled out the page from his pocket. "Look at this. I ripped it out from the book."

Henry snatched the paper. "This isn't helpful, it's only pictures and no descriptions."

"I dunno, but some pages of that book are blank, and others have symbols and figures," Moris said.

Henry mused, "How can we interpret these?" He inspected the page. "Here are our horns."

"I know, that's why I'm telling you this."

Henry gave the page back to Moris. "This could help us get back. You hold on to this paper and hide it well."

"That's not all of it," Moris explained about the Mortus Door, how it pushed him to the floor, and the awful noises he heard.

"Give me my horn." Henry snatched his horn back and gave Moris his. "Moris, don't ever go inside that door. Keep in mind, they can't know I have another horn."

Moris felt someone watching him. Behind the fence, among the trees, stood the wizard with the coat.

Moris pointed out. "Henry, look. There's the wizard I saw this morning."

Henry spun; the wizard vanished before Henry saw him.

CHAPTER 7
THE REAL SIGHT

Shortly after Tallye had left them in the front yard, Glinda came to retrieve them.

"Free time for you humans," Glinda giggled. "Er—not. If you don't play Doncelust, we'll have a problem." Her lips twitched as she smiled.

Henry still wondered if Glinda was a threat. He preferred being alone with Moris.

"You're pondering if I'm a menace, right?" Glinda asked, seeing Henry's face. "Well, you'll never know."

It seemed like Glinda was playing with Henry. Could wizards read minds? Or did she just guess by Henry's look?

"What's Doncelust?" Moris asked.

"Come, I'll show you."

The brothers followed Glinda beyond the walls and fences to arrive at a large game field submerged in the ground. Not an ordinary game. Two goals the size of indoor soccer goals stood at either end. In each of the four corners were golden rings, like ancient Earth Mayan ball rings.

Glinda explained, "If the ball enters the goal, you get one

point, but if the ball goes through one of the golden rings, you get three points. Seems simple, right?" Glinda paced in front of them, stretched her arm, and a ball flew towards her. "Well, no. We don't use a normal ball. The ball has powers and can be transformed into whatever form the player wants." Glinda's fingers danced, and the ball changed to a spikey one, then a fireball, then a lightning ball, and she added, "This is where the imagination is important. The winning team is usually the team whose creativity or imagination surpasses the other team."

"Don't you think we might die?" Henry asked.

"And? Who's going to miss you?" Glinda said with a serious face.

An awkward moment passed.

Glinda couldn't hold in the guffaw after seeing Henry's expression. "Haha! This time I'm kidding. You can be the goalkeeper. We'll give you some padding, so the ball doesn't hurt you … much."

"Why do I need to play your game?" Henry asked.

"We're missing our goalkeeper—he's working on other stuff. So if you want us to help you get back to Strakum, you'll play for us."

Henry didn't take this very well, but he thought of his mother and Maya being frightened after their disappearance. He had to get back, no matter what it took.

"Don't worry, the goalie is the safest position in the game." Glinda threw the ball to Henry, but he let it fall to the ground.

Tallye and the Veneficum players arrived with several boxes.

Glinda asked Tallye for the special uniform that would protect Henry. It would also give him small magic powers. Tallye cast a spell and a uniform hovered out of the box.

Tallye explained, "By pressing the uniform buttons, you can hurl wind, fire, bricks, water, spikes and lightning to block the ball from entering the goal."

Henry took the uniform and put it on, tapping his fingers on his shivering leg.

Moris saw his brother's amazing new magic outfit. "I want to play. It could be my first time to do real magic—kind of."

"Kid, you're too young to play this," said Glinda. "Just watch."

"Come on, let me play."

"No, Moris," Henry said. "It will be dangerous."

"You heard your brother, kid," said Glinda.

Moris grunted, stomping his foot.

The crowd gathered around the submerged field. The owls lifted some Veneficums off the ground with their claws to watch the game.

The violence of the game was beyond Henry's expectations. After the bell rang to start the game, the Veneficums howled, roared, and hit each other as they dashed back and forth after the ball. Blood dripped from their many gashes.

As the game continued, the captain of Henry's team made the ball into an ice sphere. He tossed it into the air and kicked it to score. The goalkeeper set spikes on the goal to break the ice, but then the ball changed to fire, passing through the spikes and burning the goalkeeper while they scored. Henry gawked as his team cheered. The game continued, and the ball transformed into chains of spikes, then to a cluster of snakes with huge fangs.

"Watch out!" a Veneficum yelled at Henry. A lightning ball flew towards the goal.

"What should I do? What should I do?" Henry chattered to himself. In a hurry, he started pressing buttons on his uniform. Fireworks came out, waves, rocks—useless powers. The lightning ball was getting closer and closer. Seconds felt like hours. He shut his eyes and frantically pressed two buttons, flinging out water and wind.

"Marra!" His team cheered loudly.

He'd blocked the lightning ball. Henry opened his eyes, grateful he was still in one piece. "I don't wanna play anymore; let this be the end," he said, shaking.

Moments later, Henry's vision began to blur. He rubbed his eyes, but the blur continued, and he could see neither the ball nor the players. A fireball struck him in the chest. He fell to the ground, and his brain started pounding like a drum.

"What the—ahh!" Henry shrieked, not from the blow to his chest. A searing headache cut through his skull. Half-blind, he stood up, winced in pain, and hastened to the bench. The game carried on, and only Moris noticed his distress.

"What's happening to you?" Moris asked; he sounded worried. Henry sat down to rest.

Moris whirled around for help and saw someone watching him. Hiding in the trees was the same wizard he'd seen that morning. Clad now in a black coat, he stood still and looked as if he were waiting for something.

"Henry, look there," Moris said, pointing. "There's that wizard again. The one I told you about before."

Henry didn't answer. The headache was now a migraine and left him unable to move or see clearly. Adding to his misery, his stomach stabbed with pain.

He hunched over and groaned in agony.

"What's going on, Henry?"

Now the Veneficums paid attention. They rushed to see and as they approached, Henry saw the Veneficum cloaks changing from red to dark red. Some of their wizard's faces wrinkled into a fearsome expression.

"What the— Are you looking at this?" Henry asked as he clutched his stomach in pain.

"Looking at what?" asked Moris.

Scared, Henry looked around. In the distance, the colorful, fantastic castle had changed into a dark edifice; the white clouds shifted to threatening storms, the angels of the castle had turned into demons, and the few animals around had transformed into creepy flying creatures with huge, sharp wings and big, pointed claws.

"Moris, run!" said Henry as he dragged Moris with him and dashed, terrified. He sprinted toward the forest, far from the castle.

"What are you doing?" Moris said.

Glinda chased after them and tackled Moris.

The Veneficums were paralyzed in confusion at Henry's odd behavior.

Henry fainted.

The branches rustled.

Above the leaves, the wizard with the black coat hovered. He took off his coat and, to the shock of the Veneficums, the wizard was Bastian with his blue cloak.

And from the forest poured his army.

"Incoming!" Tallye yelled. Then, with a quick incantation, she sounded the alarm.

The siren of battle.

Lucio and Iggy arrived at the battlefield flying from the castle. Both had the Veneficum symbol on their now dark red cloaks. Those with the half-symbol teleported to the battlefield. The rest of the Veneficums arrived on foot with their battle animals.

The Veneficums prepared to fight Bastian and his Milaculums.

Moris was aghast at Henry's passing out.

"You need to get inside where it's safe," Glinda said to Moris.

"No," cried Moris as she dragged him away. "I don't want to leave my brother. Let me go."

Glinda forced Moris inside the castle. Moris kicked and struggled to free himself from Glinda, but it was useless.

"What's happening?" asked Moris. Seconds later, he broke down and sobbed. "Please help my brother," he begged Glinda. He stopped resisting and was dragged through the halls up to his room.

"Did your brother drink the potion?" Glinda asked.

Moris was still crying.

"Moris?" shouted Glinda desperately. "Did he drink the potion?"

"I—I don't ..." Moris stuttered. "Yes, I think so. You even reminded him. Why?"

Glinda crossed the room Moris shared with Henry. She smelled and tasted Henry's potion.

"It's water, damn it," Glinda muttered. She changed the water to potion again and left the room, leaving Moris behind.

"Bring my brother back," shouted Moris. Then the door closed by itself.

Moris remembered this morning when the bottles trembled after the wizard he'd seen from the window had cast that spell.

He hurried to the window to watch the battle. The sun was close to setting when he finally spotted his brother, passed out on the ground near Bastian.

From Moris's perch in the castle, he could see the two armies face off—blue magic versus red magic, Bastian's army versus Lucio's army. Ready to fight.

CHAPTER 8
VENEFICUMS vs MILACULUMS

Lucio's army formed a line. Their ugly, scary tigers roared and scrambled as they were held, waiting for the signal. Bastian's army paused by the forest, ready to engage. Both armies were hesitating, waiting to see who made the first move.

"Bastian," shouted Lucio. "Turn around and go back."

Bastian glanced at the battlefield.

"We outnumber you," Lucio said. "The odds aren't on your side."

Bastian stayed silent.

Lucio knew the obvious reason Bastian was there. They had never seen a human before in Dantus World, and the special horn had appeared with them. For Bastian, it didn't matter what bloodshed was coming.

Lucio turned to Iggy and whispered, "They are not here to fight us—they want the humans and the horn. Reinforce the entrance. No one enters."

Bastian searched for the brothers, but he only saw one on

the field, unconscious. He snapped his fingers, and a shield rose around Henry.

Lucio called to the Veneficums, "Attack! Don't let them take the human!"

The red cloaks released the tigers—the thunder of the hooves on the field vibrated the ground. As they opened their jaws, flames swirled inside their mouths and formed fireballs. On command, they flung them as they roared at the Milaculums. In the sky, the owls creaked. They spread their sharp wings, aimed at the Milaculums, and as they fluttered, their feathers came out sharp as a dagger.

Bastian and his people defended themselves with water shields and iron shields. Not all of them could react fast enough, though.

They got injured.

The Milaculums paced forward slowly, parrying the attacks as much as they could. Then they lifted their spears, set them in blue flame, and flung them at the owls. Others blasted a stream of electric water to kill the tigers.

Moris howled from his place at the window, terrified. His brother was lying in the middle of the war zone. The attacks passed directly above Henry. The battlefield looked like a butchery of wizards.

Milaculums advanced to the castle.

Lucio lifted his arms to the sky and shouted, "Fogaculum, Injalum, Bitala! Fogaculum, Injalum, *Bitala*!"

The ground started to quiver, hard and continuously. Milaculums staggered as boiling smoke rose, followed by lava. The shields evaporated, and the heat started to burn their legs. Milaculums shrieked and scrambled away from the molten flames.

A long-haired woman with no cloak or symbol came running into the middle of the battlefield and cast a spell to protect herself and others from the lava. The rest didn't want to cross the lava and retreated from the battle.

Meanwhile, Bastian fought from the sky, ignoring the lava. His people were retreating, and he hadn't yet noticed.

"Bastian? Bastian?" called the cloakless woman. "They're burning, we need to retreat, and the human's shield is breaking apart."

Bastian said, "No, we must find the child with the horn." He raised his spear, looked at the sky, and cried, "Amerca Catulam Maracula ... Amerca Catulam *Maracula*!"

A menacing cloud arose, and the sky darkened. Wind blew harder and harder. The clouds electrified, and a tremendous storm broke open. Thunder and lightning took over the battlefield, and the rain put out all the fire and lava.

"Advance," Bastian shouted to his Milaculums.

The Milaculums regrouped, formed a line, and advanced as they tossed their electrified spears. Those with a half-symbol used their hands as an instrument to discharge blue flame and turned the tigers to dust.

The magic thunderstorm faded, and time began to run out for Bastian. He needed to get Henry and the other boy as soon as possible.

"Nimbulus, Nebulus, *Petraculus*!" Bastian shouted a spell again. Clouds gathered around the field, and a mist formed to block the vision of most wizards, both Milaculums, and Veneficums.

"Go to the castle," Bastian told Nabí. "Find the child and the horn."

Nabí disappeared through the fog with the rest of her team.

In the haze, Bastian landed on the ground and picked up Henry's still unconscious body. Suddenly, a red lightning bolt struck Bastian, sending him and Henry sprawling.

Bastian stood up, grunting and pulling Henry off his body. Lucio hovered closer through the fog. Bastian hurried to fly Henry's body into the trees.

"We meet again, my old friend," Lucio said with a smirk.

"Yes, indeed," replied Bastian.

"Did you think the fog would actually blind me?"

"I'd be disappointed in you if that had happened."

Lucio snorted. "It's been a long time since you've come to the castle, Bastian. What brings you here?"

"You know why, and it doesn't belong to you either," Bastian said.

"Who says? Why do you want it?"

"Same as you. Give it to me, along with the humans." Bastian wasn't in any hurry, the way he chatted in the middle of the battle.

"Is it so important that you're sacrificing your people for it?" Lucio asked. "You think they can reach the kid? Give me the other human if you don't want more deaths on your hands." He gestured at the battlefield.

"Over my dead body," Bastian said, raising his fists.

The ground beneath them began to electrify. Rocks hovered. An electric halo covered Lucio, sparkling his body, and Bastian's hand shimmered. Lucio blasted a powerful red bolt with tremendous force as Bastian thrust out blue lightning. Their lightning collided in an explosion that dissolved the clouds.

The sky was clear again.

Iggy noticed the clash between them and joined in the fight against Bastian. Lucio struck again, and Iggy teleported behind Bastian. She grasped him hard and cast a spell.

A giant two-headed snake appeared around his body, squeezing him harder and harder with its rough, dark skin.

"Farewell," Iggy said to Bastian. She left with Lucio to find Henry.

Bastian panted. He struggled against the animal's strength. The rough skin slashed him. He tried to cast a spell, but his words stuck in his throat. The animal hissed and squeezed harder. Bastian's face turned purple. His eyes flickered slower and slower until he was only semi-unconscious. Then it screeched and loosened, falling to the ground with Bastian.

"You're welcome," a woman said. She had killed the animal with a spear.

Bastian gasped for air, coughing deeply. He tossed the creature aside. He knelt on the ground, and yards away was Nabí.

"Watch out, Nabí," Bastian called.

A fireball knocked her to the ground.

Nabí stood up to find her sister, Tallye.

"Oh sister, always from behind, ever since we practiced

together," said Nabí, not surprised.

"You killed my friend, Galio," Tallye said harshly.

"Who said he's dead?" Nabí smirked.

"Walk away, sister. Don't force me to destroy you. You can't match my powers." Tallye showed her cloak with the half-symbol.

Nabí giggled. "Oh! I can see. Good for you, sister. But don't you remember what Bastian taught us? Real power doesn't just come from magic."

"Yeah, right." Tallye lifted her arm, and red sparks formed an electric dagger in the air. It blasted towards Nabí. Nabí raised a gigantic rock and struck back. Their powers collided and vanished.

The battle between sisters continued, and Tallye's attacks were relentless. Nabí struggled until she used the water from the storms to form a tornado around Tallye, blocking her view and attacks.

Desperate, Tallye tried to break through.

"You see?" asked Nabí from the other side of the tornado. "Your symbol doesn't mean you're greater than me. You lack intelligence." Cheeks flushed; she abandoned the fight and turned to Bastian.

"Bastian?" she cried. "We failed to enter the castle."

"Irrambulus," Bastian cursed. He hesitated. "Let's take the human and leave."

"Where is he?" Nabí asked.

"I hid him In the forest."

"The human will slow us down, and there are too many red cloaks," Nabí said.

"Let me worry about that."

"Like when you worried about the Draku?" She was referring to the snake he had fought.

Bastian ignored her taunt. "Call the retreat and leave through the trees. I'll be behind you."

Bastian glared at the woods, and without even a spell, Henry's body hovered, illuminated.

"The body will follow you," Bastian said. "Run for the trees."

Lucio shrieked, "Let's finish them, once and for all. Don't let them escape."

At the edge of the forest, Bastian closed his eyes and knelt with one hand on the ground. One hand faced down, and with the other he raised his spear.

"Lignu, boculus … Lignu, boculus, Petraculus!" he spelled, then dashed into the trees.

A deep rumbling echoed below the ground, which quaked. Tree roots popped out from the dirt and attacked the nearby Veneficums. Tree branches gathered, blocking any Veneficum who tried to pass through the forest.

The Milaculums escaped.

Bastian left the battle crestfallen, but with Henry. The Milaculums regrouped deep in the forest. Bastian's eyes widened at how many were injured or fallen.

"Let's go home," Bastian said in a low voice. "It will take time to heal everyone."

He opened a portal, and the Milaculums entered one by one.

Almost everyone had gone through when a hissing

echoed in the sky. Bastian looked up to find Lucio flying with Tallye as a passenger.

"Quickly, to the portal with the human," Bastian told Nabí.

She hurried to go through, and he immediately closed it behind her.

Only Bastian and the cloakless woman remained when Lucio arrived.

Lucio called, "Bastian? Who is your friend? Why haven't I ever seen her before?"

"You can ask me directly. I'm right here," the woman said. "I'm Vinghy, just an average wizard."

"An average wizard?" Lucio snorted in disbelief. "I can tell from your energy you come from another Universe." He noticed Vinghy wore a crystal ring on her finger. "It's the ring, right? This is the second time I've seen such a ring."

Vinghy smiled. "Practice makes perfect."

"And that's one of the many reasons she's called Vinghy the Mighty," said Bastian.

"Where have you taken the human?" Lucio demanded.

"He's safe," Bastian said.

Lucio sighed. "Your human is of no value; he doesn't have the horn. The kid brother will be harder to control without the brother. I need the kid's horn."

"Then give me the child and keep the horn," Bastian said.

"You know I need them both together."

Lucio tensed to attack but, in that instant, Vinghy moved faster and built a bubble-shield around Lucio and Tallye, trapping them.

While Vinghy sustained the shield, she telepathed to Bastian, *Go ahead, I can stall them and then let them catch me. I'll try to get the kid and the horn.*

Bastian was impressed she could telepath. So, he telepathed back, *It's too dangerous for you to stay with them; let me do it.*

She responded, *You're too valuable. I can't let you do that.*

Lucio and Tallye fought with the shield, and Vinghy's hands trembled from the struggle.

"An average wizard, you said?" Lucio growled.

"Go, Bastian," shouted Vinghy. "If you're still here when they break the shield, all of this will have been for nothing."

Bastian grunted. Vinghy was right. He opened the portal. "Be safe."

He vanished.

Before the shield broke, and without being noticed, Vinghy made a potion and hid it. Then she said, "I surrender. Please don't kill me."

Lucio blasted her belly with a lightning bolt strong enough to kill an average wizard, but she only passed out.

"Why don't you destroy her?" Tallye asked in a dubious voice.

"I've never seen her before, and her energy is incredible." He added, "We can use her as leverage; she's obviously important to Bastian."

Lucio opened a portal for the three of them back to the castle.

CHAPTER 9
THE DISTRESS TIMES

Days passed, and Susan kept calling the police. Each time, she explained what had happened. No one believed her story now. Maybe Robert believed her. If so, he had to be involved, or at least knew something.

Susan and Maya weren't leaving the house. They were devastated.

One morning, there was a commotion across the street. Dozens of reporters were getting down from their vans. She went out to see what happened, and immediately the reporters rushed and harassed her.

"Is it true you killed your sons?"

"How can a road just disappear?"

"Did you leave them in the desert?"

Susan froze, startled.

"Did you also kill your husband? Where did you bury them?"

Susan's eyes widened in shock, and her mouth gawked at those questions. She dashed back to the house. The crowd followed.

Locking the door behind her, she slumped down against the door and shed tears. In just a few months, she'd lost Kevin and her boys, and to the world, she was guilty.

Maya came downstairs. "What happened, Mom?" she asked.

Susan sprinted to Maya and hugged her, weeping. No words came.

Maya caressed her back. "What is it?"

"Th - they…" Susan sniffed. "There are reporters outside saying I killed your brothers."

Maya peeked out the window. The camera flashes dazzled her.

"Close the blinds," Susan said.

Susan turned on the TV again, and her house was on the news. The chyron read, *Family of crazy woman disappears — Is her daughter next?*

Susan turned off the TV, hoping this was all a dream. Maya paced to her mother and embraced her, "Ignore what they're saying, Mom."

Susan took a deep breath, headed to the window, and peeked outside. "Now everyone thinks I'm a killer." Her body felt hot as her blood surged to her head. She felt dizzy and laid down on the couch.

The phone rang. Maya went and picked it up. "Hello?"

A moment paused.

"Who is it?" Susan asked.

"It's Robert. He wants to talk to you."

"Not right now." Susan was in no mood to talk on the phone.

Then the doorbell sounded.

"Don't open it," Susan said.

Maya looked from the window, and it was the police. "Mom, I need to; it's the police."

Susan sat up; she didn't want to look weak.

"Hello, officers. Have you found my sons?"

One officer stood in front of Susan, blocking her view of Maya. "There is nothing in the area where you said your sons disappeared."

"So, what's next?"

"Well, there's nothing we can do anymore. We will not keep…"

"Maya?" Susan leaned her head to the side.

"Ma'am," the officer moved to her view. "Can you tell me again what happened that night?"

Susan stayed quiet, trying to see if the other policeman was talking to her daughter. But the officer kept demanding her attention. "Ma'am, where did your sons go missing?"

Susan rasped, "You already know that. Now leave my daughter alone." Maya was, indeed, talking to the police. She got up, went to Maya, and held her by the shoulders. "Thanks for your help, officers, but you can leave now."

After they left, Susan asked, "Maya, what did they say to you?"

"They asked about my brothers if you did something to them, if I was fine … but I ignored them, Mom. I told them to leave us alone, that we were fine, and they need to stop bothering us."

The door rang again. This time, Susan walked swiftly to the door to confront the police. But it was Robert.

She sighed. "Oh Robert, this is not a good time."

"I know, I know. But listen…" He invited himself in. "I called in a favor from the chief of police, and they're going to stop bothering you. They also took care of the news."

Susan wondered what kind of favor that was.

He saw her apprehension. "Don't worry about any of it. Just get some rest."

She said, "I don't know how to thank you, Robert. I hope I sleep, but I have to get back to work tomorrow. It's been lots of days off, and the bills won't pay themselves."

"Well then, I'll leave you alone. We'll talk more tomorrow." Robert left the house.

Susan remembered Robert lying about how he heard of her missing sons. She hurried outside to ask but then halted. *Was he helping? Or is he hiding something?* It didn't matter; it seemed he'd just helped her with a huge problem.

***

Weeks passed, and Susan sat at the kitchen table with dozens of bills in her hand. She looked one by one at all the expenses. Unbidden tears swam in her eyes.

"Maya," she called, "let's go. We have to get you to school."

"Mom," she replied, coming down the stairs. "I need to buy some books for school."

Susan went for the car keys. "Borrow them; we don't have the money."

Maya stared at the floor.

"Hey, hey," Susan said, lifting Maya's head, "I will sell a

house, don't worry."

Maya said, "I don't care about the books, Mom."

Susan pursed her lips; she knew the real reason for Maya's sadness. "We're going to get through this. I promise … Girl power?"

No response.

"Girl power?"

Maya sighed and replied, "Power girl."

"That's my girl. Let's go." It was a phrase they used to be brave after the boys disappeared.

Susan dropped Maya off at school. As soon as she'd gone inside, Susan rested her head on the steering wheel and collapsed, sobbing like a child.

She was doing what Henry did before: pretend to be strong. The only way to have a sense that everything was going to be okay was for Susan to pretend everything was getting better. But it wasn't. Maya was depressed, bills were increasing, there were no house sales. And she was devastated from inside.

Susan wiped her tears. "Be strong … be strong." She kept repeating the mantra; then headed home.

Arriving at the door, she took the keys out of her purse and glimpsed a black envelope on the floor.

"Ugh, more bills," she muttered and picked it up.

She entered the house and glanced at the envelope from all angles, then cut the upper part of the envelope. A stack of hundred-dollar bills fell out.

Susan gasped. She stared at the money, startled, and began counting it. It was *two thousand dollars.*

She hesitated, then looked for the sender. It said nothing. "What the… Should I keep it?"

The envelope had her name with her address. It was meant for her. She froze, followed by a big smile. A happy tear fell down. "I don't know who did this, but thank you."

For the next few months, the same envelope arrived every week. It took care of all Susan's money problems.

CHAPTER 10
TRUST HAS TO BE EARNED

It was night when Bastian returned to the Milaculum base. Instead of a castle, their base resembled a human mansion. The enormous house had a front and back yard, all very green with trees on the borders.

Bastian hurried straight for Henry. Inside the house, in the living room, he found Nabí and a half-symbol Milaculum, waiting for the human to wake up.

"Where's Vinghy?" Nabí asked.

Bastian shook his head. "We lost her—for now. She let herself get captured to bring us the kid and the horn."

"Why'd you let her do that? She won't make it."

"She'll be fine. She's powerful."

"That powerful?"

"She held off Lucio and your sister."

Nabí nodded and then gestured to Henry. "Should we wake him up?"

Bastian hesitated and said, "If we do that, he'll have questions, and he might fight us. I'm tired. Let him sleep, it's been a long night. Tomorrow we'll do the interrogation."

"How are you going to make him talk?"

"I'll figure it out." Bastian turned to the half-symbol Milaculum, "Domus, have they prepared the healing potion?"

"Yes, and they are treating the ones it can't heal."

"Excellent. Can you keep an eye on him?"

"We both will," replied Nabí.

Bastian left for his room, discouraged. His intentions had been the two humans and the horn, and he'd only accomplished one of those.

***

Next morning, Henry flickered awake slowly, then suddenly and totally. He jerked up, scared and confused. He twisted his head at his new surroundings; he could see again.

"Hey, relax. You're safe." Bastian grasped him and sat him down calmly.

"Where am I?" Henry asked. "Where's Moris? Who are you?"

"I'm Bastian; and if you are referring to the boy, he's in the castle."

"He's my brother. Where am I?" His upper body swayed in agitation.

"You are in my home. We saved you from the Veneficums."

"Saved me? What's going on? Why did my vision change everything I saw?" Henry gibbered.

"I'll explain everything."

"What the hell," Henry cried, noticing the other blue cloaked wizards. "You're the one who attacked us when we arrived here."

"I wasn't attacking you," Bastian said. "I was destroying the potion."

Henry frowned.

"That potion Glinda gave you was not medicine," Bastian said.

"But it allowed us to see."

"Wrong. It gave you a distorted reality of the Veneficums and their castle. That potion damaged your vision and made you see everything as beautiful in the castle. You saw the wizards in red cloaks, colored flowers, incredible animals and everything sugar and spice, but it was a false reality."

Henry hesitated, unsure whether to believe him. "You're saying everything changed to normal in the castle because I didn't drink the potion … So you're the wizard who Moris saw outside the castle from the window?"

"That's right. I converted it into water, but it looks like your brother had already taken his dose."

"And my brother?" he asked, worried.

"They took him inside before we could do anything."

"I need to go get him," Henry said. "He's in danger without me."

"We'll help, but be patient. Many of us are injured and need time to recover. Besides, Lucio needs your brother and his horn. Also, your brother is still drinking the potion, so he's still seeing everything as nice. In other words, he's fine … for now."

"For now? What do you mean?" Henry asked, worried.

"If they figure out how to use the horn without your brother, then we have a problem."

"Why should I believe you? Maybe this is all a lie, and you're the one to poison me."

Bastian shrugged. "If I wanted to hurt you, I would've done it already."

Henry hesitated. "Okay, then why am I not blind since I didn't drink their potion?" he asked.

"You traveled billions of miles through different dimensions. The Itenak blinded you."

"The what?"

"Itenak are the side effects of traveling through Universes," Bastian said. "Your blindness was from the journey, not because you're human. You didn't need the potion at all; your eyes just needed time to adapt." He paused before adding, "Truth be told, we've never seen a human travel here. Not that I know."

"Lucio said the same thing."

Nabí cleared her throat from behind Henry. "Human, I'm Nabí. What's your name?"

Henry whirled, his eyes widened. Her beautiful reddish hair swayed as her bluish eyes pierced him, followed by a freckled smile. The combination left Henry stunned. "I'm Henry," his voice quavered and gave a floppy handshake.

"Nice to meet you, Henry."

Bastian said, "We need a strategy to rescue your brother and the horn. But first, it's paramount for us to know everything about you and the horn."

Henry hesitated. "I need a break to clear my head."

Henry walked to the backyard, overwhelmed by everything Bastian had told him. In the fresh air, he closed his eyes, and an enormous sigh escaped his lips. He paused to enjoy the air in his lungs. When he opened his eyes, the bright sun made him squint. Before him was a verdant garden with enormous bushes trimmed into animals and wizards and colorful butterflies flitting among the flowers. There was no commotion, no wizards training, no noise; tranquility reigned in the garden. For the first time in the Dantus World, Henry felt something like peace.

He wondered if he should reveal the horn in his pocket.

"Henry," Nabí said as she approached from the house. "Are you hungry? We can have breakfast here in the backyard. What do you eat?"

She took the time to ask, Henry thought. "Just don't give me dirt. Can I have a human breakfast?"

Nabí smiled. "Have a seat over there. I'll be right back."

She seems nice, he thought. Yet, anyone with that beauty would seem nice. *I wonder how Mom and Maya are? Moris must be feeling so abandoned.*

Nabí returned with breakfast. "Do you think I'll like human food?" she asked, setting the tray on the table.

"Haven't you had fruits or bagels?"

"We eat mostly soil, tree bark, and gunuts."

"Do you want to taste some?"

Nabí grimaced. "Not right now. How are you feeling?"

Henry snorted. "I am lost in another world with no way to get home. My brother is alone with possibly evil wizards. I have no idea what's going on, so everything is just perfect."

"Sorry, I didn't mean to—"

"I know," Henry said, calmer. "It's just that I only want

to get my brother and go home."

"This must be awful for you. I can't say I felt the same when I lost my sister a while ago. She is a Veneficum now, but I felt awful when she turned to the other side." Nabí fussed with the tray. "We really want to help, but in order to do that, it's important to know how Moris found the horn and how you got here. I know you struggle to know who to trust, but for now, let's work on a plan to get your brother back."

"What is it with the horn? Why are you obsessed with it?"

"I'll let Bastian explain that later," answered Nabí, smiling.

"All right," replied Henry, letting the topic go. His eyes moved to the wonderful garden. No more chat, no questions, nothing as he finished his breakfast.

He peered at Nabí. Her sparkling blue eyes hit him again. He flinched as she caught him staring; he moved his eyes back to the garden. Henry waited and then glanced again, but she intercepted his gaze this time.

"What? Are you still hungry?" she asked.

Henry hummed, trying not to stare, but his eyes couldn't get rid of her.

"No, thank you," his voice quavered, then he stood up and added, "Let's talk about how we are gonna get my brother."

Nabí half smiled as she got up and took him back to the house. Bastian and two others sat on the couch, waiting for him. Henry saw Bastian's cloak. He recalled Bastian's symbol was the same as the forest gate.

"What's that symbol? What does it mean?"

Bastian said, "It represents the power of the wizards. The ones that have the complete symbol, like mine," he said, pointing to his cloak, "are those wizards who have accomplished the maximum personal level of power: magic, mind, physical and energy forces. We have reached our full potential. We control our emotions, our sentiments, and our actions; these wizards have lived long enough to have handled life according to our beliefs."

"How old are you?" asked Henry.

"To you, I appear sixty years old, but I have lived thousands of years in Dantus World. And I have lived in accordance with the way of the Milaculums."

Bastian pointed to Domus. "The ones with half-symbols have achieved two or three forces of the four. They need more experience to access their full potential. And the ones with no symbol are just beginning."

"How come your symbol is a bit different from the wizards of the castle?" Henry asked.

"You don't choose to wear the symbol or the design of it, or even the color. The cloak will do it for you, depending on your actions and how you live your wizard life. It will know what symbol you deserve and will appear by itself. Both symbols' meaning goes way back to the New Beginning Battle." Bastian hesitated, then changed the subject. "Before you arrived, I was outlining to Vikthor and Domus how we're going to get your brother. Go with them and Nabí; they are running an important errand to the village of

Zangher. They'll explain the goncelot to you on the way."

For the first time in this World, Henry had received answers. Even if none of it were true, Bastian responding to Henry built his confidence. But it still didn't prove they were the good wizards.

"Goncelot?" Henry asked.

"Yes, the strategy to take your brother. They'll explain everything while the rest of the Milaculums recover from the battle," said Bastian.

A Milaculum with long black hair and brown eyes stepped forward and said, "Henry, I'm Domus."

Henry shook hands.

"And I'm Vikthor the Bellius," another wizard said. He was tall, blond, and looked young.

"Bellius? What does that mean?"

"The kid."

Nabí grabbed Henry by the hand, leading him outside the house. "Let's go watch how Collolum wizards live in their village."

Henry's cheeks blushed as she took his hand. It had been a long time since a woman held his hand.

The four of them left for the Collolum village. As they walked, the sun changed color from yellow to red. Enormous rocks shone in different colors; trees gleamed in the light, and their leaves changed shapes.

It amazed Henry. "What's all this?" he asked, gesturing to the place.

Domus frowned. "Isn't this like on Strakum?"

Henry shook his head.

Domus explained, "Our sun changes colors as the day passes. The rocks, trees, flowers, animals and our surroundings all have energy, and when they shine, it's because their energy is active."

Henry peered around, contemplating the view. Then, the hissing of water echoed from somewhere nearby.

"Is that water? Where's it from? I don't see any rivers."

"Yes, it's water, but it flows beneath us."

Henry looked down. "You have rivers below the ground?"

Domus hummed. "Well, that's what we think. It sounds like rivers, and sometimes water blows out from the ground."

"Haven't you excavated?"

"We've tried, but we saw no water. It only sounded louder."

"The other night," Henry said. "I saw two colored moons. For us that's bizarre."

"The moons help us renew and clean our energy. Our magic powers change depending on our energy, and when it's drained, we don't have the same strength. It's said when there is an eclipse between the two moons, the energy intensifies substantially to a level we've never seen."

"How do you know that if you've never seen it?"

"That's how it works in other Universes with powers. But here, the moons have never collided, so we're not sure. How do the moons work in your world?"

Henry explained the moon has no magic effect and continued with what humans ate, how powerless they are, how the sun worked, and so on.

Soon as Henry set foot in the village, he caught the scent of fresh evergreen plants. Before him, a lush village was dotted with old, traditional cottages; some built of simple materials like bamboo, earth, and straw; others, more durable with wood and a thatch roof. The cottages were surrounded by green land, and the back of the village had a park, a small sports field, and a river.

Henry walked along the main dirt road with his guides. On one side, a wizard was helping an old lady walk home; on the other side, a wizard was carrying groceries to a woman. Kids played freely on the road. The wizards were entering houses as they pleased. Some wizards had no cloaks, and others had grey cloaks.

"Hello, Vikthor," said an old lady from the sidewalk.

"Welcome back, Vikthor," a lord wizard greeted.

Vikthor hailed to these and others as they passed.

Two kids ran up to him and pleaded, "Come and play with us, Vikthor."

"Give me a moment, and I'll find you."

Henry marveled at Vikthor's popularity. "Are you famous?" he asked.

Vikthor half smiled and stayed silent.

"What is this village?" Henry asked.

Vikthor said, "These wizards choose not to practice magic or fight the Veneficums. They prefer to live peacefully and use their magic just for their daily life. We call them Collolum wizards."

"What's going on between you guys?" Henry asked. "The Veneficums and Milaculums, I mean."

"Bastian can explain that better than me. He was there when it all began."

From afar, Henry saw a wizard dressed in … a coat? The man spoke urgently to two Collolums in an alley.

"Henry?" Domus drew Henry's attention. "Do you want to join the game?" Domus pointed out the sports field where Collolums were playing.

Henry didn't answer and turned back to the coated wizard, but he'd disappeared. He shook his head. "No, I'd prefer to know how to get my brother."

"Come on, Henry. Join me," Nabí cajoled in a sweet voice, batting her beautiful eyes. Wizard or human, it seemed flirting was universal. "Have some fun for a while. It'll help, trust me."

"Yes, Henry, give it a try," Vikthor said. "If you win, I'll buy you a kunum."

"What's that?"

"It'll make you dizzy if you drink too much. Nabí, let me know who wins."

And Vikthor left.

***

As Vikthor walked towards a house with a well-tended garden out front, a woman exited from the front door.

"Vikthor, my baby." She caressed his cheek.

"Mother," Vikthor replied, giving her a big hug. "I'm not a baby anymore."

"But your heart is. Come, let's have a drink."

As they entered, a girl came running downstairs. "Vikthor," the girl called and embraced him.

"Anori, I missed you." Vikthor kissed her on the cheek.

"You've grown too much." He held Anori by the shoulders and glanced at her from top to bottom. "Are you ready for your birthday tomorrow? What is it? Fourteen?"

"You already know. You're going to stay for it, right?"

He put his arm around her shoulders. "When have I ever missed my sister's birthday?"

Anori met his eyes with a beaming smile. "Never."

"I came with friends, but I'm going to be here for your birthday."

"Did you come a day early to do your routine with the elders?"

"That's correct. Do you want to come with me?"

"Yeah, sure."

Vikthor turned to his mother. "We'll be right back, mom."

"And the drinks?" asked his mother.

"When we get back," said Vikthor, as they left for the village nursing home.

When they arrived, the elders greeted him in a chorus of his name. "Vikthor."

Vikthor smiled and greeted each one individually.

An old woman approached Vikthor and asked, "Vikthor, did you send the present to my great-great-grandson?"

"I did. And he gave me this." Vikthor reached into his cloak and handed over a crystal collar and a picture of a young family. "He sent this for you."

A tear fell from the old woman's eyes. She took the gifts and said, "Thank you very much, Vikthor. You are so kind. There should be more wizards like you." She started to leave, then turned back and said, "Say hello to your mother. Tell her she won't beat me next time."

Vikthor grimaced. "Don't let her win, then."

The old lady winked at him and left.

Not much later, Vikthor and Anori left the nursing home. On the way home, Anori asked, "Why do you always visit there?"

"Oh, Anori," he said, placing his arm by her shoulder as they walked. "The elders have great stories to tell. They've lived long enough to understand how we should live. I listen and learn from them and try to pass it on to the next generation. Now that you're turning fourteen, it's time for you to start learning the stories."

Anori showed a tender face to Vikthor. "I didn't want you to leave us."

"I know, but I have a purpose in life, and it's with the Milaculums."

"I want to join you."

"When you're fifteen. For now, let's head back and play with the kids. I promised I'd play with them."

***

Henry watched the Collolums' ball game. Surprised, he said, "That's like our basketball."

Nabí again grabbed Henry by the hand and took him to play wizard basketball.

They gave the ball to Henry. He trotted around, bouncing it on the ground. Several wizards approached to take it back. Next, he passed the ball between the legs and dodged another wizard, then he fake-twirled and shot.

He scored.

Nabí ran over, hugging him and celebrating. Henry flushed again.

Henry felt almost like he was back home playing with normal people. There was no magic; he was just in a peaceful village.

After the game, Henry told Nabí, "Thanks, that helped me forget for a while."

Nabí smiled. "That's good. Now let's tell you how we'll get your brother."

As Nabí, Domus, and Henry walked to the village tavern, Henry watched Vikthor laughing and playing with some kids on a playground. "What's going on with Vikthor? Why is he popular?" he asked.

"Vikthor is the nicest guy you'll ever meet," Domus said. "All the villagers love him. That's why he is known as Vikthor the Bellius."

"He told me it means the kid."

Domus chuckled. "He never tells what it really means, he is very humble."

"So, what does it mean, then?"

"Good Samaritan. Because he comes home often, visits his family and the elders, and plays with all the kids. He's always helping other wizards. He helps the Collolums but never pesters them to join us."

"You have magic; what needs can you have?"

"Magic can't teach you how to be happy, to be grateful, and enjoy life. Nothing in the Universes can help with that.

There will always be anger, selfishness and other destructive emotions that we need to learn and control. Vikthor is very good at teaching this. Second, magic can't cure all disease; there are wizards who are sick, and Vikthor visits them and makes them laugh."

As Domus said this, Vikthor spotted them and yelled, "Wait for me!" He hurried to them and asked, "Who won?"

Henry said, "I want my kunum."

Vikthor embraced Henry by the shoulder and roared, "Aaah, let's go for that drink." At the tavern, Henry sat, and a drink came flying over, wedging itself into his hand. His eyes widened in surprise. "What's this?"

Nabí said, "If you desire a drink, the drink can sense it and comes to you."

Henry took a sip. Beer. "So, this is kunum? I think I like it."

Vikthor winked with a smile. "Now about the goncelot—here is what I thought. Henry makes the Veneficums believe he ran back to them to be with his brother—"

"No," Henry interrupted. "After what I saw, I can't pretend it's all good. Think of some other way."

"There's no other way," Vikthor said. "Besides, you won't be alone. We'll be outside the castle, and one of us is already inside."

"Who?"

"Vinghy the Mighty. She let herself be captured. She'll help you and your brother escape."

"On her own?" Henry snorted. "How?"

"Veneficums haven't seen Vinghy's power. When she

meditates, she has the ability to see and hear through walls. Not for nothing, she's known as the Mighty. It's very important to act normal with them; the Veneficums will be suspicious and will watch you all the time. When most of them are asleep at night, we'll signal to Vinghy. We can make the lights go off for a while, and that's when you and your brother will escape."

Henry scratched his jaw, shaking his head. "What happens if something goes wrong, or they figure it out?"

"There's that possibility, so if it happens, get out. We'll help you. But Vinghy is well trained, and I think she'll make it. If they catch you, try to look confused and scared. Say you were lost. Remember, they can't hurt your brother if he has the horn—they need the horn, and if they can't hold it, well, they need your brother."

Henry again considered telling them he also had a horn, but he still didn't say anything.

"Are you in?" Vikthor asked.

Henry rubbed his hair. "I don't know if I can handle it."

For several seconds, there was silence at the table.

"Just think about it for a while." Domus wagged a finger, and kunums came flying in.

"Aah, why not?" More beer hovered towards Henry.

After a couple of kunums, the Collolum wizards around them started singing:

Ameeee heee hoo, Amena… hena… hum
Ameeee heee hoo, Amena… hena… hum
Amena hena hum hum, Amena hena hom…
Amena hena hum hum, Amena hena hom…

Then everyone, including the Milaculums, stood up crooning, their beers raised in respect. The amber liquid dripped from the mugs as they rocked and sang all at once.

"What does it mean?" Henry shouted in Nabí's ear; the song was so loud.

Nabí yelled back, "It means to live the moment, respect everyone, and let no one take your peace. Live, love, and enjoy."

Henry mellowed with a smile from ear to ear. He wished humans abided by such a sentiment.

After a couple more beers, singing for Henry was easy. He ended up shouting along with them and spilling the kunum as he swung it. For the first time in Dantus World, he was having a good time. But he still was worried about the plan and uncertain if he could go through with it.

The song finished and Henry sat, yet still, with a lot of noise in the tavern, he asked Domus, "If I do this, you'll help us go home. Understood?"

"Yes," Domus shouted back. "Promise. We'll help you get back to Earth."

In that instant, the backdoor flew open, and the tavern fell silent. It was Tallye and three other Veneficums; one of them was the wizard he'd seen this morning in the alley. Henry supposed he was an undercover Veneficum who'd dashed to the castle to warn the others.

"Hello again, sister," Tallye growled.

"There was once a time when it was nice to see you. What are you doing here, Tallye?" asked Nabí.

"We came for the human. Let him go and no one gets

hurt."

"No, he's not leaving with you." Nabí held onto Henry, just in case.

"Whatever. The child asked for his brother and then threatened not to speak until he talked to him."

Damn it, Henry thought. *I knew he's going crazy in a panic.* He looked at Nabí and she glowered, pursing her lips. Her gaze stopped him.

"Why don't you give us Moris instead?" suggested Nabí.

"That will not happen. Give us the human or—"

"Or what? Are you going to attack us in this village?" Nabí said. "We're not in a war zone. You can't attack. Those are the rules."

"Right now…" Tallye snorted. "I don't care."

Tallye moved her hand circularly, and wind blew to gather in her palm. She mumbled something and, with immense strength, she blasted a windstorm. A Collolum staggered back, smashed into a chair, and tumbled down, thumping his head to the floor. The Milaculums' and Henry's chairs crawled backward across the floor until they grabbed a pillar. The plates, glasses and cutlery flew out, smashing into pieces.

"Give me the human," howled Tallye.

"No," said Nabí as they held strong on the pillar.

Tallye sighed and doubled the force of the windstorm. The empty chairs crashed out of the tavern through the windows, and the tables followed. Henry and the Milaculums clutched the pillar. Henry's hair and jacket billowed backward.

Tallye was relentless. She magnified the intensity of the

windstorm.

Now Henry's chair flew out, his body waving like a flag. "Help!" he yelled.

"Hold on tight!" called Nabí to Henry. "Domus, do something."

Domus groaned. He tried to make a move.

Henry's hands began to lose their grip—and his horn slowly started to come out of his jacket. He glimpsed it. "Oh, no!" he muttered.

Henry released one hand from the pillar and struggled to reach it. He fought to hold on, but it was only a matter of time. The windstorm was too strong, and his body flew off and smashed through the thin wall, falling outside onto the street. Henry's face ended up in the dirt as he groaned in pain. The horn lay a few meters away.

"What the—?" exclaimed Domus. He let go of the pillar. The windstorm blew him towards Henry, and he used his powers to shield himself as best he could.

"What the heck, Henry? You have a horn? Hide it," Domus instructed.

From inside the tavern, Tallye saw the horn. "The other horn!" she shouted. Shocked, she stopped the windstorm.

Henry saw pure rage on Tallye's face.

Domus yelled to the other wizards, "Find shelter and protect yourselves. Take cover for what's coming."

Nabí and Vikthor were still distracted looking at the horn when Tallye locked them with a special handcuff.

Tallye and the other three Veneficums went outside. She hesitated for a second, and then they fiercely and savagely reigned destruction on the village. Lightning blasted into the tavern, windstorms at the Collolums, and flame to their homes and shops. There was chaos as the village burned. Horses ran with their tails ablaze, and people sobbed in the streets. A few Collolums created shields to protect their homes, but the majority, the ones who didn't practice magic, their homes were destroyed.

Nabí and Vikthor, still inside the tavern, fought to extricate themselves from the handcuff. Domus blasted the handcuff. "Protect the Collolums!" he shouted.

Domus stayed beside Henry to protect him and the horn. Vikthor and Nabí rushed outside. Their faces fell when they saw the village burning.

"Tallye, stop!" Nabí yelled to her sister. "Look what you're doing."

"Give me the horn!" Tallye discharged flame at them, including Henry.

If Henry still had doubts about which wizards to trust, it was all too clear now.

Fortunately, Domus blocked her attacks. Defense was the only option; they were outnumbered by the Veneficums.

"What are we going to do?" Nabí yelled.

Vikthor said, "We need to take the fight away from the village."

The Milaculums grabbed Henry and dashed off. The Veneficums followed, intent on the horn.

As they sprinted in the direction of the mansion, Domus created many magical obstacles for the Veneficums. Water walls, dusty walls, brick walls and blue firewalls all blocked their way. Tallye, the most experienced of them, used her powers, but still the blockages slowed her down.

The Milaculums kept running. Nabí stayed in the rear to defend, while Vikthor ran alongside Henry. Far behind them, Tallye created a snake with a spear on its tail, aimed it at Henry, and fired.

As the spear flew towards Henry, it nicked Nabí's ear. She tried to kill the snake, but Tallye's magic was strong.

Vikthor saw the spear headed for Henry, getting nearer and nearer, a meter away from hitting him in the back ...

Vikthor wasn't a quick-spell kind of wizard and wouldn't be able to kill or block the snake. He threw himself in its path. The snake hit him with full force, and he fell to the ground.

"No," shrieked Domus. He rushed to Vikthor.

Domus cast a spell, and the snake twisted and groaned, vanishing into dust.

Vikthor gasped for air as dirt below turned red.

"Hold on, Vikthor," said Domus. "We can heal you at home."

Vikthor panted with the effort to breathe. "Don't bother ... I won't make it."

"You can't give up, Vikthor. Please, don't give up." To the others, Domus shouted, "Help me!"

Vikthor groaned, "No. Lea— leave me," he said, shaking them off.

"Damn it, Vikthor. You need to fight," said Domus, his voice loud and powerless.

Vikthor grabbed Domus by the cloak and pulled him

close. A tear slid down Vikthor's cheek. "Tell Anori I'm sorry for missing her birthday," he gasped heavily. Vikthor's eyes flickered and closed.

"No," Nabí sobbed.

Domus let out a howl of anger. He turned around, face reddened with rage, and started walking to Tallye as she finally caught up to them. Then he stopped, stood, and closed his eyes.

A dense heat descended, blazing the leaves on the ground. Henry watched, in shock, as a blue-hot point formed on Domus's fist, and with a significant force, he threw the flow of blue-fire at Tallye.

Tallye gasped in surprise. She built a shield, but it broke, and the fire slammed into her. She fell back, and the blow left her crawling across the dirt.

In his fury, Domus approached, lifting his arm and preparing to cast another spell.

Nabí begged, "Please don't kill my sister. She hasn't been herself."

Domus hesitated. Then he released a heavy sigh. "I'll not kill her."

He took out magic handcuffs from his cloak and hooked her to a tree.

"Let's go home. Henry, help me grab Vikthor," Domus said.

"What about Tallye?" asked Nabí.

"We'll take her as well," said Domus, right before they heard the other Veneficums approaching fast. "They're coming. Leave your sister; she'll slow us down."

While the men arranged Vikthor's body to travel, Nabí went to her sister. "Why? Why did you kill him? What have you become?"

Tallye didn't answer.

"Answer me! What happened to you?" screeched Nabí.

Still, Tallye stayed silent.

Nabí groaned and left her lying on the ground.

CHAPTER 11
ROYAL FAMILY

It was almost night when they returned to the mansion. Henry and Domus were streaked with blood and dirt and exhausted from carrying Vikthor's body. Nabí followed, eyes downcast. In the front yard, Bastian stood talking to a Milaculum.

Bastian turned at the noise. "What is this?" he asked, dismayed. "You were going for a drink. What the hell happened?"

"My sister happened," Nabí rasped. "She attacked us because she wanted Henry. And now his horn." She went inside the house.

The news stunned Bastian. He glared at Domus. "Explain."

Domus told him how the Veneficums had destroyed the Collolum village and how Vikthor sacrificed himself to save Henry and the horn. Domus stepped close to Bastian and whispered something.

Bastian replied, "Not now. This is not the right moment." He walked away, then turned and said gloomily, "Prepare the ceremony for Vikthor's body."

Henry waited for Bastian to leave. He asked Domus, ashamed, "What's the ceremony?"

"It's called The Koldation. We come to life with a purpose that each one of us needs to find and complete before we die. To find that meaning can take years. If we accomplish our purpose and die, our souls will be rewarded in the afterlife. If you die without accomplishing it, there is no afterlife. Yet, there are certain fortunate wizards that, if they die without completing their purpose, their body disintegrates into sand, meaning their soul will stay to finish it."

"How do you learn if a dead wizard completed his purpose?"

"In the ceremony, you'll see blue-fire. After we do the ritual, if the fire changes to green, it means he's going to be rewarded for accomplishing his purpose. Then we do a spell to send his soul into the afterlife. If the flame changes to black, his soul is doomed and his body burns, yet we still make a prayer asking The Creator for an opportunity for redemption."

"Does he ever give one?"

Domus said, "No. We keep pleading for the sake of the dead. Now, hurry to the back garden and wait for us there."

Henry didn't feel right attending the ceremony. Vikthor's death was his fault. He wanted to go to his room and sleep, like Moris, whenever he was being punished. But it wasn't his house and, out of respect for Vikthor, he had to go.

Henry wondered if Vikthor's soul would go to the

afterlife. Or had he doomed his soul? He went to the ceremony. In the garden, they'd already cleared an area for the ceremony. A plank platform for the body was ringed with sand and visible by torchlight.

As he waited for the Milaculums, an icy breeze carried music, an Uilleann Piping. Two rows of wizards marched from inside the house; between the ranks, four wizards carried Vikthor's corpse. They put the corpse on top of the plank. The Milaculums stood outside the torch ring, held hands, and began to sing a spell.

The torches lit with a deep blue fire. It rose higher and higher where it coalesced into a bubble with Vikthor's corpse inside. The sand heaved from the ground and surrounded the fire. Seconds later, it passed through the fire, changing it from blue to green. Then the chanting Milaculums cast a spell to extinguish the fire. The body vanished.

Vikthor's soul had traveled to the afterlife.

Bastian moved inside the circle where Vikthor's corpse had been. He took a deep breath and shouted with a rasping voice, "Milaculums. Vikthor, the brave and warm wizard, has left us. His sacrifice was for us. For our purpose. Remember him for what he was, the kindest wizard of all. His death should not be in vain." He looked at everyone around and said with a shaky voice, "New and ominous times are ahead. Let him be an example to all of us and let his actions never be forgotten." He paused and looked up. Shooting stars passed overhead. He added with a low voice, "Bellius, I'll take care of your family. See you in the afterlife, my friend."

Henry stood with his arms crossed and his face twisted in guilt. Bastian turned to Henry and walked towards him.

Henry flinched, afraid of what Bastian was going to say. "I'm sorry, Bastian."

Bastian acted like he hadn't heard. "Come with me. It's time you learn everything."

Bastian led him inside the house to a door. When he opened it, there was nothing inside. Henry frowned.

Bastian gestured. "This is the library. Here lies our history."

"Library? The room is empty."

"Wait."

Bastian cast a spell. The wall shook and changed to appear books in the room, as well as a painting on the black wall of Ivar with his brother Remiel and their sister Miranda.

Henry squinted at the image. "I saw those wizards in the Veneficum castle."

Bastian said, "Legend says, thousands of years ago, the first people in Dantus World were, Zadkiel and Andela Woldie."

"Legend? So, it may not be true?"

"Some of it may be true; no one knows. The divines were isolated until …" Bastian snorted. "Let me start from the beginning."

He took a breath. "Zadkiel and Andela had three children, Ivar, Remiel, and Miranda. Ivar was the strongest son but troubled. That's the wizard you saw in the Gonlu portrait. Remiel was the intelligent, bold son, and Miranda was the gifted daughter. Zadkiel could travel to other

Universes and give magic to people, creating what he named wizards."

"How did Zadkiel have such powers?" Henry asked.

"Zadkiel, one of seven divine children, created Dantus World. The Creator gave each seven divine one powerful item, and these were never meant to be used together. Zadkiel had the spear and acquired two other instruments, the horns. The horn that glows blue, faces up on the symbol, and the horn that gleams red, faces down. We believe those horns are the same as yours and your brother's."

Henry said, "Back in the cabin, my horn glowed green, not blue."

Bastian hesitated. "That's strange. We'll come back to that. After Zadkiel and Andela died, the siblings fought in a vicious battle for power; the result is the Veneficums and the Milaculums. They established that the Veneficums' cloak are the color of Ivar's horn, dark red. The symbol they have, both horns pointing down, means they seek power out of ambition and selfishness, without caring for the consequences. The Milaculums' cloaks are blue, like Remiel's horn. Our symbol, with one horn pointing up and the other pointing down, means our heart is synchronized with our brain, and it balances our way of living. We use our powers for good."

Bastian paused. "You already know the level of wizards according to the symbol."

Henry nodded.

"I was in the New Beginning Battle over the horns and the spear, fighting Lucio and Iggy, the other one with the full symbol. She was a child back then."

"Oh, he told me about that battle, but not the specifics. Lucio tried to grab the horn from my brother and burned his hand."

Bastian snorted. "I can imagine. He'll kill for its power. They've been searching for it ever since. No one has seen or heard about it until now."

"Why do you think me and my brother can hold the horns?" Henry asked, confused.

"Maybe because you're a human. That's what we're trying to figure out—how you got the horns and why you can hold them."

"Where did the New Beginning Battle happen?" Henry asked.

"At the castle. It wasn't always so scary, either. At first, it was a cabin, but then Remiel built the castle. It was spectacular, similar to what you saw when your sight was altered by the potion. Let me show you pictures of us, back when we were all together in the castle."

Bastian faced his palm towards the wall, and light came out of his hand to appear images of Miranda, Remiel and the Milaculum Family. When he changed the image to another, Henry twitched.

"Wait, turn back to the last picture."

Bastian turned back. Henry gazed at it, then squinted at it as he leaned closer. He was stunned, hand-wringing. "What the hell! That's my dad."

Bastian frowned. "What did you say?"

"This's my dad, Kevin."

"Who are you talking about?"

"That man," Henry said, pointing. "He disappeared about a year ago."

"You are confused. Maybe he looks similar to your dad, but that can't be him."

Bastian showed more pictures of the wizards and some included the same man.

Henry was insistent. "I'm certain that's my dad."

Silence descended into the room. Who would believe that the brothers' dad lived in Dantus World?

Bastian said, "I don't want to say you're lying, but perhaps you still have another kind of Itenak."

Henry frowned.

"Remember, the side effect of traveling through Universes. We don't know all the possible side effects on humans."

"I feel fine."

"Well, that's Uriel, the Omnimus, which means The Great. He's the one who left with Miranda to protect her and the spear after the New Beginning Battle. They left for a place nobody knows."

"I don't know who Uriel is, but that man is my dad, Kevin."

They paused for a moment.

"Come with me," Bastian said and led Henry outside to a small fountain. He clutched Henry's arm and cut him with a sharp stone.

"What the hell?" Henry exclaimed as he tugged his arm back. "That hurt. What was that for?"

"Put your bleeding hand into the fountain's water."

"Yeah, right. And why would I do that?"

"Do as I say, and you'll see."

Henry approached the fountain and slowly put his hand under the water. Nothing happened. The water was just tainted with blood.

"You are a human," Bastian said. "If the water had turned purple, you are a wizard."

Henry took his hand out—the water swirled and changed to green.

Bastian gasped, pulling a face. "Impossible! How can that be?"

Henry stared at the water, impressed but not saying a word.

He finally asked, "What does the green water mean?"

Bastian was frozen in thought.

"Bastian?" asked Henry.

Bastian gave a sudden jerk. "It can't be possible. Let's do it again." Bastian spelled the fountain water clear. "Put your blood into the water again."

Henry did so. A few seconds later, the water again changed to green.

"That's *incredible*," Bastian said with an enormous smile.

"What is it? Why are you smiling?"

"It means you're a—I can't believe it."

"Come on, spit it out."

"You're a descendant of the divine. Of Zadkiel Woldie."

"What? How's that possible? I'm a human; I have no powers."

"I don't know. I'm as shocked as you, yet the test doesn't lie."

"You said that my father was a wizard?"

"Yes, but you—you're not only a wizard, you're a divine."

"That can't be true. Maybe your magic isn't working right."

Bastian was wry. "Don't question my magic. Your blood doesn't lie, and turning this fountain water green means you are a descendant from the divine family. Our water combined with blood can determine your species."

Henry frowned. "Does that mean I can do magic?"

"I suppose you could if you learned. It's not easy." He added, "I'm eager to find out the truth. In the pictures I showed you, you didn't recognize Miranda. Does she look like your mother?"

"No, I only recognized my dad. I've never seen Miranda."

Henry's response intrigued Bastian.

Bastian mused, "Why Uriel wasn't with Miranda, protecting her as he was supposed to? Did she die? … I'm trying to understand how you are a descendant of Zadkiel. Even if Uriel had a family on Earth, how come you are a divine member? Tell me, what happened to your father?"

"We don't know. One day he drove to work and never came home. He was never found."

"Did he have a reason to leave?"

"No, we were a normal family. He loved my mom and us; he was the best dad. But the last thing we know is that he got in a fight with his colleague, Robert."

"Is Robert a human?"

Henry chuckled. "I thought I was a human. He looks like a human."

"A human couldn't kill Uriel. And I don't think Robert's a wizard; he might be a Warkru. But to travel to Strakum, he must have an instrument, which means a divine was involved. But I don't know, that's just a guess … Let me see your horn."

Henry hesitated but handed over the horn.

"No, put it on the table. It will burn me. Let's see what type of horn this is." Bastian cast a spell. When finished, the horn glowed blue, and several symbols appeared. "This was Remiel's horn. Look closer at the symbols and the color; these symbols are from this world. Ivar's horn has Warkru's symbols with dark red light." He added with a shaky tone, "That means your brother has Ivar's horn."

Henry noticed the look on Bastian's face. "How bad is that?"

"Moris' horn contains Warkru dark magic. Huglan altered it."

"Who's Huglan?"

"A Warkru divine," Bastian added, "After Remiel took Ivar's horn, he almost never carried it because it possessed dark energy. It may corrupt your brother's spirit if he has it much longer."

"So, what are we waiting for? Let's go get him."

"Relax, Henry. It won't happen overnight."

"How am I not going to panic if he's in danger?" Henry cried.

"Because nobody knows he's a wizard or about your divine blood. If he doesn't practice magic, the dark energy won't activate. So for now, he's safe. Besides, we don't have sufficient wizards to go now. The Milaculums haven't recovered yet, and I don't want to risk my people again without a good strategy."

Henry swallowed his panic.

"Tell me how you and Moris got the horns."

Henry explained how they'd found the horns and the reaction when he and Moris grabbed them.

Bastian scratched his cheek. "To travel through Universes, the horns needed to activate. That's odd … like you being a divine." He added, "It's been a long day. You must be tired. Let me take you to a room, and tomorrow we continue. I need to figure out who or what activated the horns."

"And how to get my brother. We need to go back home as soon as possible. My mom and Maya must be losing their minds."

"I'll think about that too."

Bastian led him to a room upstairs. As soon as the door shut, Henry threw himself on the bed.

Henry stared up at the ceiling, waiting for sleep, as thoughts sparked in his mind. *Me, a wizard! Moris needs me right now. Mom and Maya must be devastated.*

Soon, his weary eyes got the better of him, and he slipped into a deep rest.

***

Bastian walked down the hallway with thoughtful, downcast eyes. He had mixed feelings; he was crushed by the death of Vikthor, but amazed to learn the newcomer was a divine member. Then he bumped into Nabí and Domus.

"Are you okay, Bastian? How did it go with Henry?" Nabí asked.

"You won't believe it," said Bastian.

"Try me."

Bastian paused and glanced around. No one else was near. He said in a low voice, "The humans are descendants of the divine family."

Nabí laughed.

Bastian hissed at her and again looked around.

"You're right," said Nabí. "We don't believe you."

Domus said, "How's that possible? Did you check his blood?"

"Yes. Keep it quiet; no one else can know."

Nabí said, "Stop with this nonsense, Bastian. Is your magic working okay?"

"You too? My magic is fine." He continued, whispering, "Ignorant is how I feel. I can't understand how it's possible. Yet, this has to be kept secret. You don't want to know what I'm going to do to you if you tell someone."

Nabí frowned as if Bastian jested.

"I'm not kidding, Nabí."

"That's konút," Nabí replied, meaning *huge information*. "It gives us more reason to get his brother out of the castle."

"Don't you think I know that? We need another approach. Tomorrow we'll talk about it. Right now, I'm too overwhelmed."

"No kidding," said Domus.

Bastian groaned. "Let's rest until tomorrow. Not a word

about this, not even to each other. This news must not get out."

"Understood," Nabí and Domus replied as one.

Bastian left them disquieted. There hadn't been a divine wizard for centuries, and now they appeared with the dark horn.

CHAPTER 12
AND MORIS?

In the castle, Moris gasped. Bastian was kidnapping Henry. He rushed to the door and tried to pry it open.

"Glinda!" he screamed. He hit the door, yelling, though his strength couldn't match her magic.

Eventually, he slumped down against the door and wept.

He had never known such loneliness.

After the battle with the Milaculums ended, Glinda came to Moris's locked room and found him leaning on the wall, sobbing. With his brother gone, he was now afraid.

Glinda stood there in silence.

Moris raised his head. Between sobs, he asked, "Why did they take my brother?"

"Not sure. But they also wanted you and the horn." Her eyes twitched. "Maybe they will bargain."

"What am I going to do here alone?" asked Moris, despondent.

Glinda shrugged and made a tender face in sympathy.

"How are we going to get my brother back?" Moris asked.

"I must ask Lucio," said Glinda. "In the meantime, you should get something to eat."

"Why can't you ask him now?"

"He chased after your brother and his kidnappers. Maybe he'll bring him back."

A little hope appeared in Moris's face.

Going downstairs to the kitchen, Moris glanced out the window. Veneficums carried the wounded wizard back to the castle. The tigers and owls lay on the ground. The outskirts of the castle rebuilt themselves.

Reaching the kitchen, Moris sat down, gloomy. Glinda served him water and human food.

"I want to go find my brother," Moris pleaded. "Help me out, Glinda."

"I can't—I mean, we can't leave the castle," Glinda said. "I'll show you some magic tricks while we wait for Lucio or Tallye."

Moris was so glum that for the first time, he wasn't interested in magic tricks.

Not long after, Tallye and Lucio arrived with Vinghy the Mighty. She had special handcuffs on her wrists.

"Where have you been?" asked Glinda. "Where is the human?"

"Do you see him with us?" Lucio replied with a cranky voice.

Glinda grimaced. "What happened to him?"

Tallye, angry, shook her head. "They've taken the human."

"We know that. The boy saw it through the window," Glinda said.

"Are we going to search for him?" Moris asked.

The Veneficums ignored Moris, turned their back, and talked about things he didn't understand.

"Hey, kid?" Vinghy whispered. "Are you with the human we grabbed?"

"Yes," Moris said.

"Shh!" Vinghy hissed. "Not so loud."

"Why did you take him? Where is he?"

"He's safe, don't worry. I've come to get you out of here," Vinghy said. "You're in danger."

Moris frowned. "Danger? How do you plan to get me out if you are trapped?"

Lucio heard them muttering. "Hey, leave the boy alone." He turned to Tallye. "Take her to the dungeons."

Vinghy moved her lips for only Moris to read. *Find me.*

"Glinda, take the boy somewhere else. I need to be alone," Lucio growled.

Moris followed Glinda to his room. "When are we going to search for Henry?"

Glinda hesitated; her hands fidgeted. "Not sure, they didn't tell me anything. Only that tomorrow we'll figure it out."

Moris sighed. "Glinda, leave me here. I'm going to my room alone." His voice was low and despondent. He headed to his room, crestfallen.

After the brothers' father disappeared, Moris always had Henry to tell him what to do when in trouble. But this time, Henry wasn't around. And Moris was frightened and edgy.

Moris sipped the potion and threw himself on the bed. He took the horn out of his jacket and gazed at it from all angles. He gnashed his teeth in frustration and squeezed the horn. Tears trembled in his eyes. He snarled and flung the horn at the wall. In mid-air, its symbols flashed dark green, and green lightning flared when it struck the wall.

Boom! The blast knocked Moris off the bed and shook the room. The entire castle must've rattled.

Thanks to Moris, the Veneficums stayed all night on alert.

The next day, Moris jerked awake, bewildered. It was dawn. He searched for the horn and found it lying near the door where it had landed last night.

Moris picked up the horn carefully and stared at it. *How did those lights happen?* He wondered. His eagerness for some supernatural power was strong, so he tried to make the horn flash with the lightning again. He didn't succeed.

He took out the page he'd ripped from the book about the horn and the crystal rings and studied it from both sides. *Seven instruments and seven rings? Do these have powers?*

Glinda knocked on the door. "Boy, are you awake?"

Moris hid his horn and the document. "Yeah, I'm awake," he said with a frightened voice.

"Did you hear an explosion yesterday, or were you asleep?"

Moris hesitated. "What explosion?"

"Nevermind. Come out, Lucio wants to talk to you—and drink your potion."

Moris did as ordered and followed Glinda.

"What does Lucio want?"

"Don't know. We'll find out."

Lucio was with Tallye in his private study, discussing why Henry's potion had changed to water. The portrait of the endless dark room prickled Moris.

"Boy, why didn't your brother drink the potion?" asked Lucio.

"He drank it, I saw it," Moris answered.

"I don't know what happened, Lucio," Glinda said. "But Henry drank the potion; I was there. But when I examined it that night, it wasn't the potion. It was water."

"So, what the yñak happened?" Tallye asked.

Moris said, "Before the battle, I think I saw one of them outside the castle. He had a coat that covered the cloak."

"Could you recognize him?" Lucio asked.

"Yes, I think he was the same wizard you fought when you first found us," Moris said to Glinda.

"Ahh! That was Bastian," Tallye said. "Bastian must have removed the spell from the potion."

Tallye hesitated. "Moris, you keep taking the potion, so you won't go blind, or the same thing that happened to your brother will happen to you."

"Okay, when are we going to search for my brother?" He was anxious about getting Henry back.

"Not now," Lucio replied and took out a cushion. "First, show me your horn, but this time, put it on this cushion to avoid burning anyone."

"No, I'm sick of this. I won't give you the horn, and I'm not talking anymore until you bring my brother back," Moris said.

He darted out of the room through the castle without a

destination. He was frustrated and angry. What had been his dearest dream had become a nightmare. He heard Veneficums talking and approaching. Glancing around, he entered the first door he found. The two Veneficums passed by with a prisoner.

The dungeons, Moris thought. He followed them silently. The Veneficums and the prisoner entered a door guarded by two wizards. Moris hid behind a column. *That must be it.* He waited. The Veneficums came out without the prisoner, and one guard left with them. Moris hesitated, wondering how to get rid of the other guard.

Suddenly, the guard's legs began to dance. Moris frowned. *Does he have to pee?* The guard looked both ways, then rushed off.

Moris hurried and entered a gloomy hallway lit by a few flaming torches. Scared, he crept down the hall. Cells lined each side, and inside these were wizards. He kept going until he found Vinghy.

"Hey you, wizard," Moris hissed.

"Who's there? Is that the Human?" Vinghy asked.

"Yes, the kid."

"We don't have time." Vinghy came close to the door; her crystal ring shone and dazzled Moris.

Moris squinted, looked at the ring and asked himself, *Is that the ring from the page?* He shook off the thought and got to the point. "Where is my brother? Can you help me reach him?"

"Yes, I can," Vinghy replied.

"I can help you escape."

"No, it's not time,"

"Huh? When's the right time? I'm here to help right now."

"It's not that simple. I'm waiting for a signal, and then I'll escape and come get you."

Moris doubted this. "And that's easier?"

"I'm not sure what they've been telling you, kid, but they just want your horn. They don't care about you or your brother. I let myself be captured so I could take you to him. Isn't that enough?"

"Why would you do that?"

"Because … we just want to help you, humans."

"How are you gonna escape?"

"I'll figure it out. Don't worry about me. Just wait for something strange; it'll be the signal for me to escape and get you out."

"Before, why did you say I'm in danger? They've done nothing to me. Instead, you took my brother."

"The poti—" Vinghy hesitated. She said, "You're in danger because these wizards want to use your horn's power for awful things. They don't care about you and never will."

Moris took out his horn. "So this horn has many powers?"

"It's a long story, but yes."

"I knew it!" said Moris. "What do I do, then?"

"Act normal," Vinghy said. "Say nothing about this conversation, just wait for the signal and go to the Gonlu room when you hear or see it. I'll come for you."

"Okay, I'll try. I'm gonna go now."

"Wait," called Vinghy as Moris was leaving. "What's your name, kid?"

"My name is Moris. Yours?"

"Vinghy. Nice meeting you, Moris."

Moris smiled and left.

One of the guards returned to his post as Moris left the dungeon. The jailer said, "Hey kid, what are you doing here?"

Moris answered, "I'm searching for the Gonlu room. Can you show me the way?"

"You can't walk around alone in the castle."

"I'm lost, and I'm supposed to meet Glinda."

The guard nodded and gave directions.

Moris followed the first directions but then detoured outside for fresh air. As he thought about what to do, the above changed from yellow to red. He stared in confusion and asked a Veneficum who was passing by. "Is the sun changing color, or am I hallucinating?"

"It's changing. Why? Is it not normal in Strakum World?"

"No."

"Ha, weird," the Veneficum said before going on his way.

Yeah, I'm the weird one, Moris thought. The surrounding wizards in the courtyard practiced their spells. *I wished I could do magic.* At this thought, he remembered what Vinghy said about the power of the horn. He went to the back of the castle, behind a tree where no one could watch him, and took out his horn. He moved his arm like he was throwing a baseball, and said, "Lightning."

Nothing happened. He tried again and said, "Throw ray." Again, nothing. Moris even rubbed the horn as if it were a magic lamp. His eagerness to create magic fed his anxiety.

He was patient, especially so for his age. He recalled what had made the horn glow, and it occurred to him to repeat the conditions—which had included Moris getting angry.

He thought about his lost father and his kidnapped brother. Then it happened: dark energy sparked through his body to the horn, which began to glow dark green. Moris's body stiffened, and his eyes flashed red.

"What the—?" said Moris, astonished.

Moments later, the energy faded.

"No," he shouted, wanting the magic back.

He rested for a while with his back on the trunk. He rubbed the horn, imagining he could use its powers. Footsteps approached and he hid the horn.

Tallye and Glinda arrived.

"Where were you, boy?" Tallye asked, her voice calm. "You can't be alone outside the castle; it's getting dark."

Moris looked up. "I was taking in some fresh air."

"Come, Lucio wants to talk to you."

"Not until you find my brother."

"We found him, but the Milaculums won't let me bring him home. I told them you were worried, and that you wanted to be with your brother. They didn't care and attacked me and held your brother hostage."

"Why should I believe you?" he said, standing up.

"I know your brother has the other horn, the blue one, and the Milaculums are holding him hostage for it."

Moris' eyes widened. *This is bad. Now they could hurt Henry for it,* he thought. "Who told you that?" he asked. Henry would never say anything about his horn.

"I saw it myself."

Moris frowned, not sure what to think. "Okay, why did you say it was the blue one?"

"We know there are two horns, the red one which you have, and the other according to legend is blue."

Confusion paralyzed Moris. He'd never seen Henry's horn glowing blue—only green when he grabbed it by mistake back in the library. Yet, he couldn't say anything about that.

Who should he believe, Tallye or Vinghy? Furious and desperate, he growled, "I want my brother."

In his pocket, the horn glowed dark green. Its light spilled out so they all could see. Tallye and Glinda gaped.

"Boy," Glinda said slowly. "I can tell you're scared. You know we also want to find your brother, right? Let's go to Lucio to determine how to bring him back."

Moris sighed, "I need a moment to think." Moris walked away to cool down. *If they want the horns, they must find my brother.*

He turned back and said, "Okay, I'm going to listen to what you have to say."

They headed to the castle and entered a room Moris hadn't seen before.

"Where are we?" asked Moris.

"This is the Latium room," said Glinda. "The ample space you see in the center is for the wizards to fight and practice magic, like a fighting ring."

The walls had bookshelves filled with books, and to the side were tables and chairs.

At the back of the room, Lucio sat reading a book. "Moris, come and join me," he said calmly.

As Moris neared, he could tell Lucio was exhausted by the dark circles under his eyes.

Lucio said, "I'm going to need you to tell me all about the horns you humans have."

"We already told you," Moris said. "Henry gave it to me as a souvenir."

"Don't lie to me, boy," Lucio growled. "I'm losing my patience. If you want me to help you find your brother, tell me who you are and how you got the horns." He was so angry his eyes bulged.

Moris was an eleven-year-old kid. Anyone could get rid of him easily. So he told them about the cabin that was like the castle and how they teleported to the Dantus World.

He watched Lucio ponder in silence.

Then Lucio cast a spell, and a book from a shelf hovered towards him. He opened it and showed a picture to Moris. "Is this the cabin?"

Moris's eyes widened in surprise. "Yes, how is there a picture of it in the book?"

"The cabin was here before the castle was built. This is a very ancient picture, where Zadkiel and Andela raised their children."

Moris had no idea what Lucio was talking about. "Who are Zadkiel and Andela?"

"They were the founders of all the wizards. But it's a long story, not for today." Lucio added, "Why didn't you tell me this before?"

"We were scared. We didn't know who you were or what's going on."

Lucio stood up and paced, rubbing his chin. "Neither do we. It mystifies me how you were in that house. It doesn't exist anymore. And it never existed in your world."

"Well," Moris said, standing up from his chair. "Now that I've told you everything, it's time for you to help me find my brother."

Lucio looked down at Moris. "You're right. We'll search for him. Just let us figure out how." He turned to Glinda and said, "It's late now. Take the boy off to bed."

CHAPTER 13
THE POWER OF HEART AND MIND

Henry watched from above as a man sat among the trees and by a fire, rubbing his arms. He squinted at the man. The man got up and looked at the sky. Henry's eyes widened as he gasped. "*Dad?*"

Henry jerked awake, in shock and breath heaving. He wondered if it was a normal dream or a dream like the one he'd before about the cabin. He shook his thoughts off, rubbed his eyes, and stretched with a yawn. His sleep was fitful, his mind electric. It's not every day you learn you're a divine member or even just a wizard. It was as if he lived someone else's life.

He left the room. As the door thumped closed, a voice echoed from behind, "How has the wizard slept?"

He turned. Nabí smirked at him.

"So, you know?" Henry asked with a low voice. He was still dazed.

"Yep. Only me and Domus. You must keep it a secret; no one else can know."

"I didn't even want to know." Henry scooted away.

Nabí chuckled and scampered behind Henry. "Where are you going?"

Bastian appeared from the end of the hallway. "Morning, Henry."

Henry looked at Nabí. "At least he called me by my name," he sneered, walking past Bastian.

Bastian frowned at Nabí, confused.

Nabí shook her head, smiling. "He's processing the news."

Bastian followed Henry and said, "Join us for breakfast."

As they went to the dining room, Henry glanced outside and saw wizards hugging enormous tree trunks with white leaves. "What are they doing?"

Bastian halted Henry. "Watch closely."

Henry stared. A white dot glowed in the middle of the tree trunk. The air blew towards the tree, and the light grew wider with each passing second until it illuminated the entire tree. Now the tree gleamed. Seconds later, the light trickled down onto the Milaculums' bodies, and they jolted.

Henry boggled. "What just happened?"

"Our energy needs to be cleaned and renewed. We receive some of it from our environment, including the trees."

"Haha … what?" The laughter came out unexpectedly.

"You laughed as if I'm the crazy one, but you have much to learn. Come on."

Henry stayed and watched. The wizards shivered as they received the light.

"Henry? Are you coming?"

Henry caught up and entered the dining room, where Domus was eating alone.

As Domus saw Henry, he lifted his hands and, with a grin, greeted him as a king. "Good morning, our Dortalus."

"Dortalus?" Henry asked but didn't care to know. He just wanted to get back home.

"Yes, it means Liberator. Your divine powers can help us with the fight."

Henry laughed.

"Sit, please," Domus gestured to the chair beside him. "Henry, how come you never knew you're a divine?"

Henry shrugged as he sat down. "I asked myself the same thing."

"You being a Royal wizard, it's our responsibility to wake the wizard inside you," said Domus.

Bastian made a face as he moved the chair to sit. "I don't know. It's very dangerous and takes a lot of time, which we may not have."

"Let him try. He may be a quick learner," said Nabí as she grasped soil.

"Yeah, Bastian," said Domus. "Henry can surprise us."

"Wait," Henry cut in. "You're talking as if I want to learn magic. What if I don't want to?"

This stunned the wizards into silence.

"I just want to get Moris," he said. "And go back home."

"You're joking, right?" said Nabí, astounded. Her hand with the soil froze before her mouth. "We're telling you that you can be powerful, and you just don't want it?"

"It's in your blood," said Bastian.

"You can do magic," said Domus.

"You are a divine descendant," said Nabí.

Henry shrugged.

"You're destined to be a wizard," Bastian tried to convince him. "The horns found you for a reason—I just need to find out how they activated. But you could be one of the greatest wizards of all. Your potential power could help us defeat the Veneficums, bring back Moris, and help you find your father."

"Will I be able to rescue Moris and reveal the truth about my father?"

"Certainly," Bastian said. "With your powers unlocked, it's possible."

Henry mused. "Okay, but I'm doing this for my family. I don't want to get involved with your war. I only want to get home with my mother and Maya as soon as we get Moris. I can't imagine what they're going through. Are we clear?"

Bastian's face dropped. "Yes, we're clear," he said.

"Okay then, what are we going to do?" asked Henry.

Bastian slid his chair back, stood up, and said, "Get ready; it's going to be a long day. Come with me."

Henry and the other Milaculums followed and left through the backyard.

"Where are we going?" asked Henry.

"You'll see," replied Bastian.

As they got closer, he saw gigantic trees upside down, with the crown on the ground, the branches clustered, buried, and holding the tree. Instead of having roots at the top, it had another crown of leaves. In the middle of the tree wall, there was a road.

"This is the Epiculus Forest," said Bastian, walking below the canopy.

The colorful flowers released a smoke with a refreshing scent to relax and feel peace. Different color trees: white, orange, red, green and pink, the branches with different leaves and colors.

"This is amazing," Henry said as he followed.

The Bollys, the round, and hairy animals that had wings, long ears and small legs, flew towards Henry and licked his body in greeting. Henry grimaced.

"Now you've met the Bollys," Bastian said.

"I've seen them before when we arrived."

"It seems they sensed your divine blood … These are the cute ones. I hope you never meet the ugly ones."

As the Bollys passed on their way, a beautiful pink flower rose from the ground and opened its petals. Teeth appeared, and it roared as it ate a Bolly.

"What the hell?" Henry asked, bewildered and scared.

Bastian laughed. "The Epiculus Forest is the strangest forest in all the Universes. You'll see the strangest creatures, plants, and animals here. Even for us. All the villages connect to this forest."

As Bastian spoke, a snake slithered in front of Henry. Instead of a tail, it had a second head. Across the clearing, a turtle ran and chased what looked like a rabbit, but with eyes on their ears, and the ears moved like stalks. From afar, frogs ran on two feet and jumped to eat the tree leaves. On the left, a squirrel of the size of a lion was eating nuts.

"Oh my god. This is crazy. Is it dangerous here?"

"For the wizards, not that I know. But never forget this is the most mysterious Forest in the entire Universe."

Moments later, they arrived at an esplanade surrounded by more trees. Bastian took out some sand from his bag and sprinkled a circle on the ground. Domus and Nabí moved away.

"Henry, get inside the circle and hold your horn with your hand outstretched," Bastian instructed.

After Henry stood in position, Bastian lifted his hand to the sky and uttered, "Glokus, Apartulus." The sun changed to dark green, and the sky became dark. Colored lightning appeared in the upper atmosphere, and thunder rumbled. A black cloak formed in the air.

"I've never seen a cloak like that," said Nabí, confused.

"Zadkiel descendants' cloaks differ from ours," said Bastian.

The cloak flew towards Henry and attached itself around his neck. He squirmed as an incredible sensation swept through his body. "My God, this is incredible," said Henry. His horn pulsed a green glow.

After a few seconds, the tingling disappeared.

"I can't sense the energy anymore. I want it back."

"It went dormant," said Bastian. "But you still have it inside you. You just need to learn how to draw that energy out, then you can train to your full potential."

"How can I learn that?"

"Ahh … now you want to practice magic? Where is the human who doesn't want power?"

Henry lowered his head.

Bastian gave a small laugh.

"Don't I need a magic wand?" Henry said.

Bastian groaned. "I will ignore what you just said. Your powers don't come from a wand or a spell; they come from your energy. You first need to sense the energy within. Where you put your attention is where you put your energy. To do that, you need to concentrate on one energy spot of your body."

"Energy spot?" asked Henry, bewildered.

"Ugh! Humans…" Bastian huffed in obvious frustration. "Your knowledge of the Universes and its energy are primitive. The most important energy spots in each body go from your spine to your brain. You concentrate on the spots to elevate your aura and energy. Remember, where you put your attention is where you put your energy, so once you find your energy, transfer it to one place—it can be a horn, spear, or a hand—"

"A magic wand?" said Henry with a smirk.

Bastian smiled. "Yes, it can be a wand or any other instrument. After enough practice, you can draw out your power without a specific spell."

"What about my horn?"

"Yes, the horn will help you increase it exponentially. That's why divine members have too much power. But, for the sake of all, you need to learn well while you are here, and that's what I'm going to teach you. Now that you are inside the circle, connect with your body and locate your energy. Transfer that energy to one spot and say, 'Contráculus.'"

Henry stood, one foot in front of the other. He then cast the spell, "Contráculus." Nothing happened. He tried again, "Contráculus," and nothing happened. He shook his head.

Bastian said, "Concentrate on the spots. Sense and expand your energy."

He tried again, many times, and every time he failed.

"I can't do it. I sensed nothing, I'm just a human."

"With that attitude, you won't achieve anything," said Bastian. "You are a divine. Clear your mind and listen inside your body."

Henry closed his eyes and tried to clear his mind.

As his thoughts started coming in, his body began pounding, his face flushing. Dark energy flew through him. With that energy, he suddenly let out a howl of anger.

Bastian, Nabí and Domus looked at each other, stunned.

"Henry?" Nabí said, frowning. "What just happened?"

"I don't know." He paused. "The moment I closed my eyes, I had terrible thoughts of Moris being alone and the death of my father."

"You let your thoughts control you, which leads to feelings which you might not want to have and forces you to react in a way you may regret. Negative thoughts are dark energy. Observe your state of mind and body, be conscious all the time, and control your thoughts. Didn't they teach any of this on Strakum?"

Henry said, "They teach us math, grammar, Spanish, science … the basics."

"Basics?" Bastian sneered. "How do you connect your body, mind, and soul?"

Henry shrugged.

"That's shamefaced! Mastering yourself is the most important lesson. Connecting your body, mind and soul is a universal supernatural power; you feel complete, providential. Anyone in the Universes can achieve it. But if you let your thoughts or emotions consume you, you cannot transcend."

Bastian went on to explain that Milaculums didn't have schools. What they could research and learn in books didn't need to be taught by someone else—it was all self-study.

"Henry, we need to train you to connect body-mind-soul. You can't be a good wizard if your emotions dominate you. A strong conscious mind is what will control your actions, your life. We'll practice in the library," Bastian said. "I'll hide your cloak so no one finds out your secret, and you hide your horn."

They went to the empty library, where Bastian offered a chair and told him to sit down.

Henry sat.

"That's how you humans sit down?" Bastian asked scornfully. "Sit up straight."

Henry jerked, stiffened, and sat as told.

"Now, close your eyes and take a long breath." Bastian waited. "Repeat this many times."

As Henry followed the instructions, his muscles loosened, and his mind went blank. He relaxed. It was time to begin the training.

Bastian stood behind Henry and spoke in a low voice. "I'm going to do a memory spell on you. You will relive all the experiences you've had in life. It can be joyful or painful. You'll do this so we can see how mind-strong you are and how you react to your emotions. Let's begin."

Bastian took out a wand—knowing full well Henry might laugh if he opened his eyes—then touched Henry's head and said, "Animoslu."

Henry's mind lit up. His internal world became more real than his external world. He went deep into his subconscious operating system. In this state, he stopped listening to his thoughts and suddenly saw images of his family. Then he went into a hypnotic state. His body was resting, half asleep but awake. He was conscious in his subconscious mind. Last, he switched from Theta to Gamma state, and his body's energy rose to the brain, feeling an excitement within him. The brain went into a super-conscious state, where he had the ability to relieve his experience.

The first memory was a woman carrying three newborn babies. Some unfamiliar people, one dressed in black and the other wearing a hood, came in and took one of the babies from the woman, which made her sob. Henry recognized the woman as the old lady from the cabin, the caretaker, but younger.

Another memory appeared. He saw himself as a child playing the Universe Game with his dad. He smiled, his eyes moistening with tears.

He then flashed back to walking on the street when a bunch of other kids approached him and knocked him. He tried to avoid that experience by changing to another.

Now he was in school, on recess … two kids bullied him

before pushing him and throwing a ball at his belly. He felt rage and, again, changed the memory. Negative experiences kept coming, though, leaving destructive emotions in their wake.

Henry couldn't control himself and he grew heated. With his face red-purple, he grabbed his chair and smashed it against the wall.

He addressed Bastian with his fists up. Just when he was about to knock Bastian down, Bastian shouted, "Stop! Master yourself."

Using magic, Bastian stopped Henry in his tracks.

Henry woke up exhausted and bewildered. "What the—what happened?"

"I warned that you'd relive your experiences and emotions."

"I didn't expect it would be that real."

Bastian chuckled. "Look what you've done. You didn't control your mind."

Bastian showed Henry the remains of the chair.

It surprised Henry. He recalled his mother telling him not to withhold feelings but wasn't aware he had so much anger inside him.

"First wizard lesson. Emotions are a record of the past, and the solution to your problems is not to think within that emotion; it's getting beyond yourself and getting beyond the emotion. Most of your reactions are unconscious because you program your mind to do it that way. The sentiment you have is repeated, again and again, over your life, and your mind programmed it to do things without reasoning. So, you need to be aware of your emotions to avoid the reaction."

Henry said, "How can I do that?"

"If you can't explain your behaviors or feelings, it's because you're not connected to your brain. The more you understand what you're doing and why you're doing it, it'll be easier to change your being. Besides, you've yet to release your burden of the past, forgive others and yourself, and most importantly, be grateful."

"I can get everything you said, but forgive myself?" Henry asked, confused.

"That's correct. You may regret something you did or didn't do and continue to suffer from it. So, when you meditate as I told you, you'll be aware of your emotions and have the opening to unburden and control yourself. Change your negative thoughts to a positive one, then give thanks for what you have, and your heart will open to a greater love with an incredible force. You need to practice by experiencing all your emotions. Let's do it again. Sit on the chair."

Bastian used his magic to repair the chair and clean the room. They started all over again.

Henry's memories appeared. This time there was a memory of his dad yelling at him. Henry reacted furiously and destroyed the chair again.

Bastian woke him up. "Come on. Calm your heart and focus on your emotions. Let's do it again."

They kept going again and again… Each time, Henry reacted the same way—he couldn't contain himself. He was desperate and recalled his mother saying to him: *the grief will consume you.*

"Last round," Bastian said. "But this time, I will go inside your mind, as if I'm in your memory, and guide you when the emotions appear. We'll go step by step."

Bastian spelled "Animoslu Moriaelus."

The first memory was Henry playing with his dad.

Bastian smiled, stunned to see his old friend Uriel as Henry's dad. He asked, "What emotion did you have playing with your dad?"

"Joyful," he answered with a grin from ear to ear.

"Good. Next one …"

An angry memory appeared, one where he was beaten up by other kids. Before Henry reacted in the usual outburst, but Bastian's yelled, "Stop."

Henry contained himself.

"Look into yourself and tell me what you feel," Bastian asked.

"Enraged. I want to hit them all."

"But why are you angry?"

"Because I couldn't defend myself. I felt powerless."

"Now you realize why you are angry, and with this, you can control your emotion. Find the spot in your body where you feel this, your belly, heart, stomach, wherever it is; then breathe slowly, and move that feeling out of your body. Exhale it. Next, open your heart with gratitude."

Henry breathed slowly, feeling the anger in his heart. He inhaled deeply, transferred the emotional lump into his mouth, and exhaled it. His body relaxed, and his mind traveled to no place, no past or future concerns—only the present moment. He gave thanks for being alive. His anger was released, and his chair survived.

"Excellent," said Bastian, nodding.

Bastian sent Henry to another unpleasant memory, when his dad yelled at him, sending him into his room for punishment.

"I can see you were in trouble," Bastian said. "How do you feel now?"

"That I disappointed Dad, that I'm not good enough for him and I'm angry with myself," Henry replied.

"Perfect, you are conscious of what you are feeling. Remember to figure out why you feel this way to define the emotion you're having and to avoid a reaction. You are the only one who can interpret it. Repeat the same to release a change in your emotion."

Henry felt this lump-emotion in his belly and repeated the process.

Bastian watched how Henry's tears struggled to get out. Henry was holding them back because the memory was about his dad's disappearance.

"Now, what emotion are you having?" Bastian asked.

In a cracked voice, Henry said, "Devastated, alone, and angry."

"I can understand being devastated and alone, but angry?"

"Maybe it's because we had a tremendous fight the day before he disappeared. I'm just angry with myself that I couldn't say sorry, or that I love him."

A silence emerged in the memory, and Henry still held

back his tears.

Bastian tried to comfort him. "This is where you need to forgive yourself. I know your father, Uriel—well, Kevin. And I'm sure that he knows you love him, and he forgives you. You are his son. Now … *wake up*."

Bastian and Henry got out of Henry's memories.

A cascade of tears came from Henry. He gasped convulsively, releasing his burden of the past and the grudges he'd had. His mom would be proud.

"Congratulations, Henry. That was very good. The act of observing those states of mind and body means you're conscious of your actions, but you still need to show me you can do it alone."

Henry took a deep breath and exhaled through his mouth, calming down his body.

Bastian approached, put his arm on his shoulder, and said, "Now, be grateful for everything you possess, and you'll open your heart and connect your mind-body-soul. Above all, believe in yourself. With this, you'll use your energy to your full potential."

"How am I going to do that?" Henry asked.

"You'll learn how. Come with me."

CHAPTER 14
THE POWER TO BELIEVE

Bastian led Henry outside the house. To the left, away from the Epiculus Forest, rose a great hill. He took out a lens, but instead of glass, it had a transparent stiff-paper type. With that, he looked directly at the sun.

"What are you doing?" Henry asked.

"Do you want to try it?" Bastian stretched the lens to him.

Henry took the lens and saw through it. The sun had nine lines attached around it—one of them was smaller, and symbols bore beside the lines.

Bastian explained, "The lines show how long the day is. Today we started with fifteen lines, but tomorrow we might start the day with eight. A line is an hour, and as the time passes, the minutes or symbols change and the line gets smaller."

"My God, that's completely out of the ordinary," Henry said.

Bastian took back the lens and pointed at the hill as he

said, "Reach the top in forty minutes."

Henry laughed. "Come on, man. It'll take me at least two hours."

"You haven't even tried, and you're already giving up. At least try it."

Henry sighed. It was impossible. With his negativity at the forefront, he didn't try hard and the obvious happened— he didn't get there in time.

In an hour, they were only halfway to the top.

They kept going. At one point, Bastian turned, and Henry was bent over, panting with his hands on his knees.

Bastian handed him a bottle of water.

"Told you, I can't do it," said Henry, gasping as he clutched the bottle.

"Let's still finish," said Bastian. He turned and kept moving.

Henry grunted and followed Bastian.

Another hour later, Henry arrived at the top. He crouched, his legs trembling and his lungs looking for air.

Bastian, watching his distress, issued quite possibly the most inappropriate command, "Give me a hundred push-ups."

"Hell no," refused Henry. "I can't even move."

Bastian cast a spell, and a bubble shield locked them both at the top of the hill. He said, "Henry, the only way to get out of here is when we both finish the push-ups."

Henry tried to get out. He bumped into the shield and tumbled. "Irrambulus!" he cursed in the wizard language. Getting up, face reddened, he cried, "Let me out."

Henry felt impotent, like a child being locked in his room. "Let me go, or I'll punch you in the face," he said, rushing toward Bastian and looking for a fight.

With a flick of his wrist, though, Bastian cast a spell and froze him like a statue.

Henry screamed and fought to extricate himself from the spell.

"That's enough, human," yelled Bastian.

Henry stopped. He'd never heard Bastian call him human.

"Stop behaving like an animal and master yourself," said Bastian.

"How is this gonna help me do magic?"

"Wizards need stamina and self-confidence. Use what you learned in the library."

Henry hesitated. "I'm mad and tired."

"I know. But consider that your tantrum made you waste energy. If I hadn't stopped you, you would have drained all your energy. Now, let us finish."

Bastian released Henry from the spell.

For Bastian, it was a daily routine. He completed the pushups, then sat down in yoga style and closed his eyes as he waited for Henry to finish.

Meanwhile, Henry despaired. "How is this gonna help me believe in myself?"

"Don't waste time and energy," said Bastian with his eyes closed. "Finish it, so we can leave. It's getting late."

"That's your problem; you locked us up here," Henry said and kept counting the push-ups.

Bastian remained sitting and quiet for half an hour.

"Ninety-nine. One…" Henry gasped, "hundred." He sprawled out on his back.

The shield disappeared.

Bastian opened his eyes and stood up. "How do you feel?" he asked.

"Really?" Henry chuckled darkly. "Great. Do you want me to do another hundred push-ups?"

"Making jokes now? I can cast another spell."

Henry sighed and shook his head.

Bastian smirked. "My question was not whether you are exhausted or not. We know the answer to that. I was referring to how you feel about accomplishing the work?"

Henry thought it over. "Good. Even though it took forever." He stood up, "Sorry about my reaction before, wizard. But that wasn't cool."

"Wizard?" Bastian asked.

"Well, you called me human before."

Bastian nodded with a half-smile. "We can head back now. Tomorrow, we'll work again."

As they headed back to the house, Henry saw the colored mountains in the distance and asked, "What is it with those mountains? Why are they colored?"

"Each mountain has a different kind of energy. You see them colored according to the color of the trees' leaves and energy. Remember earlier when you saw a Milaculum receiving energy from a tree? Well, the white light you saw is the energy of peace. The red trees give the energy of love; the orange is the energy of strength, the green is the energy of confidence, blue of courage, and so on. You can also choose to receive good energy or dark energy. And the tricky part is that it becomes addictive."

"How's that?"

"How can I explain …" Bastian said. "If you use the trees constantly, two awful things happen. First, the trees can die if you drain too much energy from them. Second, the more you use them, the less you can increase your energy by yourself. Your energy can't depend on a tree; it's just for a little push once in a while. You must learn to elevate your energy by yourself."

"And how do you know if it's dark or not?"

"Negative thoughts, darker the energy. Positive thoughts, positive energy."

Henry considered this as they walked in silence the rest of the way. Nabí was waiting for them when they arrived at the house.

"What took you so long?" she asked.

"Bastian couldn't keep up," Henry said with a wink.

"We're not finished, Henry. What sport do you like?" asked Bastian.

Henry paused and sighed in sadness. "Archery. My dad taught me when I was a kid. We'd still go to the range every week, right up until he disappeared."

Bastian stayed silent for a moment. He then created a bow, an arrow, and five targets. He said, "Okay, you must place the arrow in the center of the objective at five different distances. If you fail to hit the center of the target at any distance, start over until you put all the arrows in the center on your first attempt."

"What is it with your challenges?" Henry sighed.

"What is it with your whimpering? Try it before you say you can't."

Henry hit the first target and the second. On the third, he missed. He snorted and started over. Again, he made the first target but then missed the second. "It's more difficult than expected," he said.

He kept trying and couldn't make it all the way through. The farthest he achieved was the third target.

Henry threw the bow down and said, "I'm done."

Henry left towards the house.

Nabí hurried after him. "Henry, you can't give up. Your brother needs you … we need you." Her voice was sweet as she tugged his arm. "The key to success is to concentrate and sense the surroundings."

"Every shot is different from the last one. I bet that not even Bastian can do it."

Bastian cleared his throat. Henry hadn't noticed Bastian following.

"Yeah, I bet even you can't make it," Henry repeated.

Henry watched Bastian grab the bow and the arrow. Bastian gazed closely at the targets, then closed his eyes. He breathed deeply for a few seconds—Henry thought Bastian would open his eyes—but then, unexpectedly, he shot the arrows with his eyes closed.

Henry goggled. Bastian had hit all of them in the center. He put down the bow without saying a word.

"Best keep trying, Henry," Nabí said.

"What?" Henry's face dropped. "How did you do it?"

"It's not about whether you can see the target," Bastian said. "It's about the ability to sense everything around you by listening to their energy. You don't need eyes to see. You need to have a clear mind to listen to the environment, the wind, and the targets. Then you'll have a clear shot."

It was getting dark, and for a human, it had been a long day.

Bastian took out a bottle and said, "Drink this potion and get some rest. It will help you recover fast. Every day, we'll repeat until you succeed."

Bastian turned to leave. He stopped and said, "Henry, before you sleep, remember all the things you accomplished today. You climbed the hill, completed the pushups, and hit the third target—it doesn't matter if you finished the challenges differently. Just think positively about the little things you've done."

Much later that night, after a meal with the Milaculums and a nice bath, Henry lay in bed thinking about Bastian's words.

I'd never climbed a hill or done a hundred pushups. It felt good … The third archery target was hard, but I can do better and hit the next ones.

After a quiet moment, he realized that what he had done—it was, in fact, an accomplishment. Such positive thoughts, he sensed, were the beginning of a new Henry.

***

As promised, Bastian and Henry repeated the same exercises the next day. This time, they climbed the hill in an hour and did the push-ups more quickly. In archery, he reached the fourth target. And before going to bed, again, Bastian said to Henry, "Remember the minor achievements. Think positive."

Each day Henry was faster than the last, until one day at the beginning of the hill Henry looked at Bastian and said, "Ready … one, two, three." They bolted into movement, kicking up grass in their wake. Henry put all of his energy into propelling forward, but Bastian pulled ahead in the first half of the hill.

"I thought you were ready," said Bastian, looking back at Henry.

Henry smirked and kept his speed steady.

At the halfway point, Henry speeded up and passed Bastian. "Keep up, old wizard," he sneered.

Bastian half smiled, then moved his hand as if doing a spell.

"Nu-uh," said Henry, shaking his finger and rushing up the hill.

He finished the hill in thirty minutes and did the push-ups faster than Bastian.

"Well done," said Bastian, patting his back. "Now for the archery challenge."

There, Nabí and Domus were shooting arrows. Henry greeted them and picked up the bow.

"Okay, Henry, stare at the target carefully and then close your eyes. Clear your thoughts, your mind. If a memory comes in, ignore it, and focus on your breath. Listen to your surroundings, and sense the targets."

With Bastian guiding him, Henry analyzed the target before he closed his eyes and cleared his mind. He located his energy spots. The wind stroked Henry's face, the birds sang, the trees swayed. He sensed the energy all around and the targets.

With his eyes closed, he aimed for the first target and shot the arrow. It struck the center of the target. Henry sensed it, so he continued to shoot the next target, and again he hit the center. Then he shot the third and fourth targets and also hit the center. He'd made it to the final target.

Henry paused for a moment. He then breathed slowly with concentration. He held out his arm to sense the air and its speed, then prepared to shoot. He stood still, sensed the wind, moved his arm to the side, and shot.

A spontaneous gasp echoed.

Henry opened his eyes. The last target wasn't even in the same place. Although it'd moved, he'd hit all the centers of the targets.

"Yeah," Henry yelled in excitement. "I did it."

Bastian, Nabí, and Domus were dumbfounded.

"Oh, human!" That was the second time Bastian had called him human, but this time was friendly. "Congratulations. You did it, even when the last target moved."

Nabí went and hugged Henry. "You did it."

He flushed. She then tugged him by the arm. "We need to celebrate with a drink. Let me take you for a kunum."

They all headed to the house bar to celebrate.

"Impressive, Henry," said Bastian. "You've completed the tasks better than expected. Now, do you believe in yourself?"

Henry nodded, grinning.

"That's the power of your mind," Bastian said. "Now it's time to master yourself and control your reactions when angry."

"I'll try harder." Henry drank his kunum. He paused. "Bastian, when can we get my brother?"

"In another day or two. Tomorrow I'll have a report on how the Milaculums are recovering."

"It feels like it's been months without my brother. Hope you're right, and Moris isn't in danger."

"If something happened to him, we'd know about it. So … no news is good news." Bastian lifted his kunum. "Salute, Henry. Enjoy your drink."

Their glasses clinked.

After some drinks, Bastian and Domus stood up to leave; Bastian said, "Tomorrow you'll learn how to do magic. Don't let Nabí keep you awake too late."

Nabí smiled. "Yes, sir. Good night, Bastian … Now go away."

Henry saw them leaving and said with sadness, "I miss my brother so much. I just want to get back home with my family."

Nabí sighed. "Family," she said in a low voice.

He then dared to ask, "How is it you and Tallye are on opposite sides?"

Nabí's face saddened. "I don't know. Even after our parents died, she was a wonderful sister. We were as thick as thieves, inseparable. They called us *Tanna*, which means beloved sisters. One day, we had a silly fight practicing magic, and she ran away. She never came back to us and since then has joined the Veneficums."

"That's sad," Henry said as he caressed Nabí's hand. "I can't imagine fighting against Moris or any of my family."

"It saddens me to talk about it. Tell me, have you picked out a wizard name?"

"Do I need to have one?"

"Well, you are a divine, and Henry is not a divine name. I have an idea: you can be Henriol," she suggested, teasing him. "Our parents choose our names. You have the opportunity to think of a cool wizard name."

Henry offered a shy smile.

They talked late into the night. And as Nabí talked, she ran her hand through her hair. Her bluish eyes hypnotized Henry. She even touched him from time to time.

Henry's heart quickened, and butterflies soon followed. *I can't fall for her;* Henry kept thinking. *She lives in another Universe.*

Before it got awkward, she said, "Oh! Look at the time. I don't want Bastian to kill me. You need to rest for tomorrow. Prepare to be a wizard, Henriol."

She stood up, then hesitated. She put her lips to Henry's ear and whispered, "Goodnight, my wizard." She kissed him on the cheek.

Henry's blush deepened. "Goodnight Nabí. See you

tomorrow."

Henry went to bed feeling cheerful and with an unknown sensation: self-assured. He knew that he'd accomplished something he'd been struggling with: to believe in himself. Now it was time to learn to master himself and save his brother.

CHAPTER 15
THE DEAD WOODS

In the morning, Moris opened his eyes and was startled by Glinda staring at him. "What the hell?"

She sat on the bed.

"Did tears fall in your sleep?"

Moris ignored her question. "Why are you here? Are we going for my brother?"

"Not yet."

Moris groaned.

"You want breakfast?"

"If it's a human breakfast, then yes, please."

"Drink your potion first."

They headed to the backyard for breakfast. A seat was already set for Moris with a bagel and eggs. *Now they're getting it,* Moris thought. Veneficums nearby were sitting on the grass, legs crossed.

"What are they doing?" he asked.

"Watch closely."

A skinny and starving wizard approached a seated Veneficum. The wizard's hand hovered above the

Veneficum's head. An orange light came out of the wizard's hand, penetrating the Veneficum's head. The Veneficum shivered.

Moris pulled a face. "What just happened?"

Glinda said, "We all possess energy for our magic. To increase our power, we need to renew our energy. Those wizards are transferring their energy to us."

"So that's why they looked so withered?"

"Yes. They are addicted to the tree's energy."

"I don't know what that means."

Glinda sighed in exasperation. "Our trees possess a lot of energy, but it's extremely dangerous to use them often because then we become dependent on them and unable to increase our energy by ourselves. But if another wizard transfers the energy to us, we don't become addicted and dependent."

"It seems to me you're enslaving other wizards for your purpose."

Glinda shrugged. "You think I care what a human thinks?"

Moris changed the subject before he made her mad. "Glinda, what should I do while you decide when to look for my brother? Can I go outside the castle?"

"No, you can't be outside."

"What can I do then?"

Glinda hesitated. "Do you want to try the special Doncelust suit your brother used?"

"Awesome!"

They headed to the backyard, and Glinda gave Moris the suit. She explained again how to use it. There was no ball or a goal, simply the suit to try. He cautiously pressed a red symbol, and fire came out of his glove.

"Wow," he said with a jerk. Then he grinned from ear to ear. "That was awesome."

He lifted his right arm and pressed a white symbol. The force of the wind he blasted tumbled him down.

Glinda giggled. "Are you ok?"

Moris got up with a grin plastered on his face. "Oohh, I'm excellent," he said. "I'm doing magic for the first time."

"Don't get too excited, kid. Take it off; I need to leave."

"Aw," Moris lowered his head. "Do you only use the suit for the game?" he asked, hoping he could wear it all the time.

"No. It can allow us to fight without consuming our own energy. There are lots of beasts in the forest."

"Can you fight a wizard with it?"

Glinda paused. "Go back to where we had breakfast. Tallye will get you there."

Moris did as he was told.

Minutes passed, then an hour or more. Bored, he remembered Vinghy in the dungeon. He went to find her.

He peeked down the hall at the guards standing like statues. He pondered and then paced towards them.

"Hey kid, what are you doing here?" asked a guard.

"I'm supposed to meet Tallye, but she didn't show up. I'm searching everywhere."

"You can't be down here."

"What should I do? I can't wait forever."

The guards looked at each other. One said to the other, "I'll look for her. Stay here."

Moris half-smiled. *One more to go,* he thought.

He waited, more and more impatient, as every moment reduced his chance to talk to Vinghy. Suddenly, outside the window, a tiger bit an owl. The owl got angry and wedged its claws into the tiger.

The guard went to the window to look. "What the … Stop." No one was around outside to stop the fight. "Stay put, kid." He said and dashed off.

Moris bolted inside the dungeons. "Vinghy, are you here?"

"Moris, we don't have time; I can't control the beasts too long."

"What? Are you—"

"I told you, we don't have time. What do you want?"

"I want to get my brother. Let me help you get out now."

"We need to stick to the plan. Be patient."

"Aren't you here to help me? It doesn't look like it—they told me your people took Henry hostage. Why would you do that?"

"Moris, be careful whom you trust. These wizards are not who they appear to be. Be cautious, for they will deceive you."

Footsteps approached.

"Leave before they see you," said Vinghy. "Stay alert for the signal."

Moris nodded and left the dungeon. *I will trust the one who helps me first,* he decided.

When the guard returned, Moris was sitting out in the hallway. He said, "I couldn't find Tallye, and you shouldn't be walking around alone. Go back to your room."

Moris nodded and left, but he detoured to the Wooly room, the library, and entered.

He hurried to the pedestal and the crystal case. He held out his horn, glancing at it from the corner of his eye and hoping it would flash. But nothing happened. He got closer to the glass, and it didn't open by itself this time.

He tried to force it open and failed. He punched the glass and hurt his hand. "Ouch!" he said, shaking his wrist.

Next, he pressed his palms on the glass and pushed it—er, tried to. "What the heck, why doesn't it open?"

Moris gave up and went to the hidden door—the Mortus Door. Scared, he expected to hear the roaring; but silence was the only thing he heard. Intrigued, he stretched his hand, touched the door handle. He paused, remembering Tallye's warning that no one ever came back. He took his hand off.

As he was heading out of the library, he saw through the window a light flickering outside the castle. Drawn to it, Moris went to the gate and looked around, making sure each Veneficum was busy. He took the opportunity and dashed away towards the light.

Walking in the forest, the ugly Bollys came in and flew aside him. "Get out of here!" he scared them off. As he said that, a two-headed, two-legged beast with an enormous nose ran like a human through the woods. Moris hid behind a tree. *Why the hell did I leave the castle?* He peeked at the beast. By that time, it was close to the light.

The beast was his size with bent legs, but all of a sudden, the beast unfolded its legs and stretched to ten feet tall. It then leaped high and grabbed a nut from the sleeves of the tree and ate it before it wandered off.

Moris waited for it to get far ahead. His ears heard nothing, so he left the safety of his tree. Suddenly, the beast was before him with his back crouched, looking down at Moris and spitting at him. It muttered something Moris couldn't understand.

Moris froze, stunned and frightened. *Don't move,* he repeated to himself. He even didn't want to clean the spit from his skin.

One of the beast's two heads went behind Moris and the other in front. Sweat trickled down Moris's forehead. The beast sniffed Moris and scowled.

Moris closed his eyes. *I'm going to be killed by a monster.*

Seconds after, nothing happened. Moris opened his eyes and saw the beast was small again, and a crystal ring flashed on one finger. It was identical to Vinghy's.

The beast left, mumbling, "Manjura Tanjara Myla…"

Moris sighed in relief and continued toward the light, wondering what the ring meant and what the beast had said.

Soon, the forest turned to dead, fallen trees. He looked closer, and some trees had holes in their trunks. Moris startled.

He lightly tapped one tree, and it sounded hollow. It then collapsed into pieces. The light ahead blinked faster and stronger. He hurried towards it, to the edge of the forest, and halted. Yards away, dozens of wizards embraced trees while the trees glowed intensely. Moris hid himself carefully, not wanting another tree to disintegrate because then the wizards might notice.

The trees gleamed in different colors before flowing into the nearby wizards' bodies. The wizards shrieked as this happened, but Moris couldn't tell if it was from pain or excitement. The process repeated itself until each tree had no more light and fell.

Moris was aghast. The wizards embracing the trees were just as haggard as the wizard he had seen earlier.

Moris felt a lump in his heart. *Are the Veneficums using hundreds of addicts to get energy?* He couldn't believe what he was seeing and didn't like it. He rushed back towards the castle before anyone noticed he was missing. In his haste, an addicted wizard bumped into Moris.

The wizard grasped him and gibbered hotly, "I can't get enough, I can't get enough. Help me! I can't stop…" Without meaning it, the wizard transferred his energy to Moris.

Moris gasped and shuddered in contentment; the horn in his pocket shone dark red.

"Hey you," shouted a Veneficum to the wizard. "Get back to the trees." He then turned to Moris and went for him in a rush. The horn dropped to the ground.

"Let me go," scrambled Moris.

The Veneficum dragged Moris through the woods. Abruptly, the two-headed beast appeared and smote the Veneficum, thrusting him a mile away. Moris fell behind the beast.

The Veneficum got up, shook his cloak back, and blasted lightning. The beast squinted and darted towards it. Yards away from the lightning, he leaped, grabbed it, and with a twirl he flung it away to the sky.

"What the—" said Moris.

The Veneficum gaped.

The beast unfolded his legs again, gaining immensely in size, and mumbled something. Roots came out from his fingers and flew from his hands toward the Veneficum.

The Veneficum gasped and darted away. The roots followed and caught up with him, hitting him in the chest.

Moris was horrified at the death.

The beast folded himself up again and headed for the horn. Moris froze in shock.

The beast grabbed the horn, examined it, and then gave it to Moris.

"Run. Go back," the beast said.

"Wha-wha-what are you?" Moris stammered.

"Run, *now*."

Moris fled back to the castle, scared and unable to fathom what happened. At the gate, he stopped and panted with his hands on his knees.

"Moris?" Tallye said. "Where were you? You can't be outside."

"Where was I? Really? I waited for hours for you. Did you expect I'd be sitting around doing nothing? I went exploring around the castle."

"I don't care. You can't be exploring by yourself. Get inside."

Moris couldn't stop thinking about what he'd seen. *Why didn't the beast burn when it touched the horn? But boy, it felt amazing while I received that energy.*

Moris's curiosity got the better of him. "Tallye?"

"What is it?"

"Something's going on outside the castle."

"What do you mean?"

"Well, I mean the addicted wizards and the trees."

"You said you walked around the castle."

Moris shrugged.

Tallye glared but said, "The addicted wizards also need to renew their energy. For us to help them, we drain their energy so they can receive it fresh from the trees. If they stay too long with the same energy, their hearts stop."

"You're telling me you're saving the wizards from death? That's really odd," said Moris, skeptical.

"That's how it works here on Dantus World."

"I saw a something else—a beast, I don't know, but it had two heads and—"

"Ah, yes. He's not a beast, he is a cursed Manzokan from the Manjara Universe. His own people cursed him."

"Why?"

"I've no idea. The Manzokans visited us weeks ago, and the cursed one traveled secretly, for he was a prisoner and escaped. We've tried to capture and send him back, but he's hiding in the Epiculus Forest."

As they arrived at the gigantic main door, the imprinted map and symbols on the ancient wood changed right in front of Moris's eyes.

Tallye saw his reaction and explained, "The map shows lost cities and those that are not in a specific Universe. The symbols help us find that city here in Dantus."

"I don't understand."

"There are places that move through Universes and appear from time to time. We call them the lost cities because we don't know where or when they're going to appear. When a map appears on the door, a lost city has arrived on Dantus."

Moris asked, "How many lost cities are there?"

Tallye shrugged. "I don't know. Since we took the castle, the map and symbols have changed many times."

"You said 'took the castle'?"

Tallye pretended not to hear. "Oh, look, it's getting late. We'll eat dinner, and then you get some rest."

Moris wondered why Tallye dodged the question.

After a quick meal, he headed to bed, thinking about the craziest experience he had and how badly he wanted to be with his brother.

CHAPTER 16
THE GONDMUND STAGES

For the next three days, Moris followed the same routine. He woke up, had breakfast, and asked Glinda when they were going to get his brother—she had no answer. He visited the dungeon, but the guards never left. He walked around the castle and killed time, bored as hell.

On the fourth day, he changed his routine and headed to the library. He approached the book, but nothing happened. Then he passed by the Mortus Door, and a voice whispered: Manjura Tanjara Myla.

Moris froze in place. He turned to the door and heard the words again.

"Manjura Tanjara Myla."

Moris frowned. *That's what the Manzokan beast said.*

"Manjura Tanjara Myla," it repeated louder.

This isn't a coincidence, Moris thought. He debated entering, but remembered again Tallye's scary warning. *Hmm, let me just take a peek.*

Moris opened the door delicately. His eyes turned red,

hypnotized, and he was pulled inside. The door closed and his eyes returned to normal.

"*No*," shrieked Moris. He turned and tried to break the door down, to push through it. His hands searched for a hidden button, but before his eyes, the door disappeared and the room became dark.

"What the heck have I done?" He groaned. "What am I going to do? Am I never going to get out?" He was stunned, hand-wringing, and his heart raced at the thought of never seeing his family again.

Moris's horn began to glow. As soon as he touched it in his pocket, a section of the floor opened to reveal stairs leading down.

With no other option, cautiously, Moris walked down the stairs. The hallway was dark and cold. He took out the glowing horn and walked down between the walls. At the bottom, a dazzling light shone. The walls had become transparent to reveal life in the castle.

Moris spun to watch everything. He saw Tallye in the backyard practicing magic, Glinda having lunch, Lucio reading a book. Moris shouted for help, but no one could hear him. He saw Vinghy in the dungeon; she seemed to be meditating. Then she turned towards Moris.

Moris was startled. "Vinghy? Can you see me?"

"Irrambulus," Vinghy cursed. "Moris, why the hell did you enter the Mortus Door?"

"Vinghy? Can you see me too? How do I get out?"

"You can't; it's impossible unless—"

"Unless what?"

Vinghy's mouth shut because a guard passed with another prisoner. She telepathed Moris, *What have you done? You are doomed.*

"Thanks for the hope."

"The only hope is you differ from the rest."

"Help me!"

Moris stopped seeing Vinghy, and the scene switched back in time until he saw himself walking to Maya's room. He gave her a birthday present. She smiled and hugged him. The scene changed again. He was making dinner for his mother, who sat devastated after his Dad's funeral. Moris went to her, rubbed her back, and left the food. "You need to eat, Mom."

The scene switched back to the castle.

Moris looked for Vinghy. "Vinghy? Vinghy?" he shouted.

She didn't respond. *Well, maybe I can find my own way out.*

Moris followed the hall and the wall became dark again, and the horn lit up. He moved forward until he arrived at another room. All of a sudden, the entire wall started to project unfamiliar places and people. He guessed it might be another Universe altogether.

The people rode an animal with a bent neck and long-snouted head, with a bony armour, and a curled prehensile tail. No arms or legs, but it seemed to fly over the ground. It might look like a … seahorse?

Curious, Moris went to the wall and reached out to touch the animal. Suddenly, the wall waved and sucked him through to the other side. The force pushed him to the ground. He groaned, got up, and—

"Aahh!" he screeched and dropped to the ground again, for a herd of the huge animals flew towards him.

Seconds later, nothing happened. He peeked out, and the animals were passing through him. He glanced around. He'd arrived in a desert with snow. The flying creatures were ridden by shirtless people whose heads were painted. A man on an animal who appeared to be the leader—because he had necklaces and rings on his fingers—turned to Moris, squinted at him, and stopped his animal. The rest continued riding. Moris wasn't sure if the man could see him.

The man approached. As he got closer, he asked, "Who are you? How did you come here?"

Abruptly, the scene changed. Now Moris was on a rocky, red, hot mountain; steam and smoke surrounded him. The world was on fire, and it seemed a dead place.

Moris was grateful when the scene changed again. He was in the middle of a street surrounded by buildings, but darker. The people around were all dressed in black with a trench coat.

The trip continued to another dark place. Beasts and demons flew around, fighting with angels. Moris did not want to be there either.

And then he landed in the worst place of all: Earth. Moris watched his mother preparing dinner for Maya, both gloomy.

"Mom? Maya?" he shouted desperately.

Maya twitched as if she'd heard.

Before he could shout again, he traveled back in time to

his tenth birthday. His Dad came and gave him a nintendo game. Moris thanked him but didn't seem too excited.

"What is it?" his Dad asked.

"No, no. I liked it, but I preferred—"

"Money?"

"No, Dad."

"A magic class?"

"I do like magic, but…" He paused.

"You want a smartphone and be a blogger?"

"Dad, I don't want money or fame. I want you to teach me archery like you did with Henry."

His Dad sat beside him and set his arm around his shoulder. "I can do that," his Dad said.

Moris returned to the black room. Tears in his eyes.

Lonely, Moris wanted to tell Henry about all he'd seen. He remembered no one had ever told the story of going back through the door, and his fear returned.

The wall stopped projecting places, so Moris continued exploring. There, the horn stopped shining. No light, no transparent wall or TV wall, no noise, no room. Literally nothing. Moris tried to run back to where he could see Vinghy, but there was no way back or forward. It was an endless black space.

I'm done. Why did I open the door? Why? Moris sat down, terrified and sobbing.

After minutes that felt like hours, a hoarse voice said, "Moris Walcar…"

Moris jerked and glanced around. "Is someone there? Help me please!"

"I sense you, divine Moris," the hoarse voice said. "A unique soul." The words came from nowhere and everywhere.

"Divine? I'm just a human. How do you know my name? Who am I talking to?"

"Souls don't mind who you are. Here there is no who, or where, or when, or what."

"Then what is this place? How do I get out?"

"Those were not rooms; they were the Gondmund stages. It shows the potential in you. The first stage projects the pureness of your heart. He who has a pure heart can see beyond. The second stage shows the pureness of your mind. He who reaches a peaceful mind has no limits. And the third stage is nowhere and everywhere, no time, no place, or space. This is where your soul is tested."

"Oh man," Moris lamented. "So I'm dead."

"Those who do not have what it requires on each stage are doomed. This last stage is where your soul, and your connection with it, are measured."

Moris kept his mouth shut.

"Each soul is enlightened through the thoughts and deeds of one's life. The Universes have disregarded the true meaning of living. Those we see are worthy of having a divine power, they survive."

"What are you talking about?" He just wanted to get back to the castle.

"You'll learn through time." A small bottle appeared before him out of the void. In it, he could see a small snake with deadly-looking fangs. "Drink this bottle."

"What? No. It has a snake in it."

There was no reply.

"Hey, are you there?" Moris paused, waiting. "What are you talking about? Drink a snake? Don't leave me."

Moris groaned.

He glared at the snake. *What am I going to do? Drink the snake, really? Ugh!*

He grabbed the bottle and opened it. He examined it from all sides, then slowly brought the bottle to his mouth. He closed his eyes and drank. It tasted like acid.

Moris's body disintegrated into colored light. He traveled through endless space at lightning speed. He flew over planets, stars, constellations, and even Universes until he reached a white potent light.

Moris jerked awake with a gasp.

Looking around, he recognized Lucio's study by the painting on the far wall of an endless dark room.

He went to the painting and stared at it. *What the hell happened?* He thought, followed by a shrieked, "I'm alive. I'm alive!"

He hid his horn and quickly got out of Lucio's den.

Downstairs, he ran into Tallye. "I'm alive, Tallye. I'm alive."

Tallye frowned. "Are you feeling okay, kid?"

Moris calmed down so as not to raise suspicions. "Never mind. I'm great."

"Okay … your human food is ready."

Moris kept thinking about the Mortus Door and the Gondmund stages during dinner. He didn't understand anything the voice had said about divine power or the soul connection.

"Hey, kid," Tallye said, interrupting his thinking. "What's on your mind?"

Moris couldn't tell her about his adventure, so he lied. "I was thinking of my brother. I miss him. When can we find him?"

"We still have no answer."

Moris' patience had gone. "I want my brother." The horn glowed so intensely that even his clothes gleamed.

Tallye gasped in shock. "Wow, relax kid. Are you sure you're okay?"

"No, I'm not. It has been days without my brother. How do I know he's still alive?"

"He's alive, don't worry. We'll look for him; we just need to find the right moment. I see you've finished your food. Why don't you get some rest? You look tired. We'll talk tomorrow."

Moris didn't mind being alone in his room. He had a lot to think about.

In bed, Moris kept musing about the experience behind the Mortus Door. He couldn't figure out what the voice was trying to teach him. It had said, *You'll learn through time.* Whatever that means.

CHAPTER 17
UNLEASH THE ENERGY INSIDE

Henry opened his eyes and stayed in bed, looking at the ceiling. He yawned, stretched his legs, arms, and sighed. An electric charge flew through his body.

If anyone entered the room, they would have seen a grin plastered on Henry's face and also sensed the energy of greatness and self-confidence around him.

Soon he got up, dressed, grabbed his horn, and headed to the kitchen to have breakfast. No one was in, yet there was human food on the table. He served himself breakfast as if he were at home.

Not long after, Nabí came in. "What do you call that food, Henriol?"

"Really? Still going with Henriol?"

"Well, think about a name, or we'll stick you with one." She grinned.

"By the way, I slept well. Thanks for asking."

"You read my mind. Did you use your powers for that?"

"Yeah, sure."

"Okay, tell me, how do you feel?"

"Great. Ready to learn magic," he said.

She sat beside him, looked into his eyes, and said, "Remember to be conscious of controlling your reactions. Bastian is not always around in your mind. Open your heart with gratitude, and practice every day, so then it'll become routine. Don't let the anger take the best of you."

"Thanks, Nabíus," Henry said.

"Aaaa, so now you are giving me a name?"

"Tit for tat."

Nabí frowned. "What does that mean?"

"Equivalent retaliation."

"Sorry for interrupting your flirt," Bastian said as he arrived. "Finish your breakfast, you'll need your energy today." He joined them at the table. "Pass me the bread and eggs."

Henry grimaced. "Have you tried human food before?"

"There's always a first time."

Bastian served himself some of the human food. He took a fork and stabbed the bread with it.

Henry laughed. "You eat dirt with your hands, but use a fork for bread?"

Bastian paused. He removed the bread from the fork and popped it in his mouth. "This actually tastes good," he said and continued with the eggs. He liked those too.

"Nabí, do you want to try?" asked Bastian.

Nabí hissed, "Thanks. I already ate."

Bastian finished his plate and said, "That was tasty." He got up from his chair and went for a backpack. "I have your cloak in here. Nobody needs to know who you are, or you'll put yourself in danger. Follow me." Bastian grabbed some papers and stuffed them into the pack, then went outside.

As they left through the front gate to the Epiculus Forest, Henry glimpsed beside the bushes a force-field of light with divisions and Veneficums inside. Out of curiosity, he approached.

Nabí followed, explaining, "This is our jail. No magic can be done in these cells. There is no escape for the Veneficums inside."

In one of those cells sat a wizard that Henry recognized from his very first moments in Dantus World. "Was he here when I arrived?"

"Galio? Yes."

Galio was sleeping but plainly quite alive.

Confused, Henry said, "They told me he sacrificed himself—that you killed him."

"Sacrificed himself?" Bastian interrupted. "Another lesson: don't trust a Veneficum. He didn't sacrifice himself. Tallye left him so she could escape. As you can see, he's well taken care of. We seek peace between us and between Universes. We don't kill, even if they are our enemies. Unless we have no other choice."

"Did you say Universes?"

"Oh Henry, there's so much you humans don't know. You're the most isolated among all living creatures."

"I've heard that before," he said. "What are you going to do with Galio and the others?"

"We don't know. For now, we'll keep them here. The

Veneficums must stop killing for power." In a lower voice, he added, "And with you as a divine, your powers can help us."

"Don't get your hopes up," Henry said. "I told you, I want nothing to do with your battles. I just want to get to my brother and get back to my family. And maybe learn the truth about my dad."

"Having a divine with us would be so helpful. But it's your choice. Either way, we'll help you get your brother and figure out if your dad is alive."

They headed on into the Forest. Henry watched a winged animal approaching them. It had no hair on its wrinkled body but had a toothless mouth, short legs, and long, hairy ears hanging down.

"What is that ugly thing?" Henry asked.

Bastian said, "That's the ugly Bolly."

The ugly animal flew towards Bastian and mumbled something.

Bastian held the ugly Bolly and transferred a light to it. The ugly Bolly changed to its normal shape.

Henry frowned. "What was that?"

"He asked me for energy."

They kept walking as Henry thought about it.

"Okay, Henry, this is perfect," Bastian said. "As you can see, there is peace and silence all around. Here it should be easier to find your energy and reach your potential. Let's see what you've learned. Once more: open your heart, it's all in your—"

"Brain. Yeah. I know," Henry said. "Clear your mind,

breathe slowly. I've heard it so many times; I think I know how."

"Well then, put it into practice. Believe in yourself."

Henry wasn't sure if he was ready. Instead, he asked, "Do I stand back and say Contráculus?"

"Not too far, I don't think you can hurt us," Bastian said wryly. "Remember the steps you need to take."

Henry took out his horn and cloak from the backpack and stepped back. He closed his eyes and breathed deeply. He paid attention to the various spots of his body. His energy warmed, tickling him. He then focused on his surroundings and lifted his arm, and the horn glowed green as his energy flowed into it. He hesitated, then said the spell. "Con … tra … cu … luss."

Nothing happened.

He repeated the spell many times. Each time the horn glowed green, but nothing else happened. Everyone, including Bastian, was disappointed.

"This is a waste of time," said Henry. "Maybe my human half is holding my wizard half back?"

Bastian said, "Something isn't right. Why does the horn glow green? It should be blue." He went for the backpack, took the documents out, and scanned them, searching for something.

Nabí watched Bastian frowning. "Bastian?"

"Henry, show me your horn," he said.

Henry held it out to him.

Bastian gazed at the horn from one side to another without touching it. He hovered his hand above it, levitated it, and cast a spell. "Abnemlus Montalum."

Green lightning surged around the horn. Henry's fingers curled reflexively around it. His body shuddered and quivered while the lightning traveled from the horn into his heart. His heart pounded as his body began to hover. His torso stretched upwards hard, his hair spiked while his eyes turned completely white. Henry screamed. Then his body returned to normal and stopped hovering.

Henry gasped for air. "That was incredible. What happened?"

"Someone blocked the wizard inside you," Bastian said. "That's why it was green light."

"Who would do that to me?"

"I was going to ask you the same. Maybe your father did it so you could live a normal human life."

"But why wouldn't he want me to be a wizard?"

"It doesn't matter now as I've awakened the wizard inside you. Now you can try again."

Henry ambled away from them. He took time to breathe. He closed his eyes, focused on his energy spots, and sensed the surroundings. He then stretched out his arm and said, "Contráculus!"

He opened his eyes and to see some small rocks rising from the ground, hovering in the air. He got excited, which distracted him, and the rocks fell. "I did it! I lifted a rock!"

"Congratulations," Bastian said. "You can say you've done your first magic. Let's try again, but aim wider and try to keep them floating this time. Do what you did in the archery challenge. Close your eyes, breathe slowly, sense the energy."

Henry said, "You're just like my dad. He repeated everything."

Bastian snorted but didn't say anything.

Henry tried again many times, and the result was the same. Only a few rocks lifted off the ground. He groaned in despair. His face reddened.

Seeing Henry come close to another emotional meltdown, Bastian was about to stop him, but Nabí touched Bastian and said, "Trust him. Let's see what happens."

Henry gnashed his teeth and struggled with his frustration until an unbidden memory with his father appeared. His father picked up the bow Henry had thrown and gave it back to him. "Be patient, Henry. Nobody does it right the first time." Henry closed his eyes and, with several deep breaths, cooled his anger. He had mastered himself without help.

He breathed slowly for several minutes, listening to the environment: the rustle of the trees, the birds singing, the burbling water. He focused on his energy spots until he felt them pumping, and all the noise disappeared.

Energy spread through Henry's legs and arms and ran down to his fingers where blue lightning sprouted. It radiated all around him, and his hair stood on end.

Henry cast his spell again, lifting both of his arms straight, "Contráculus!"

A loud boom rumbled through the ground. The earth vibrated as the rocks and sticks rose to hover. Moments later, everything dropped to the ground, and the lightning around Henry's body disappeared.

Bastian said, excited, "Never in my entire wizard life have I seen this much power in a novice wizard. What you just did takes a lot of training and experience. How did you do it? Your potential is our hope. We cannot win the war without you."

Henry opened his eyes. He didn't need to see what he had done; he felt everything. He dripped with sweat as if he'd run a marathon. "It was because you repeated the tutorial every time," he teased.

Nabí laughed.

Henry said, "But look at me, I'm exhausted."

"No kidding! You look like you came out of a pool," Nabí said.

"I need some water,"

"You are a wizard—create some. Try *Utremqua*."

Henry said the spell, but he was tired.

"Don't worry, it's your first time," said Bastian. "Magic powers don't work without energy. Eat dirt, you'll recover fast."

"No way, I'm not eating that. Make me something human."

"Don't whine," said Nabí. "It tastes good and it's super healthy. Our soil has all the nutrients and minerals our bodies need."

"That's right, your body."

"You're a wizard too," she reminded him.

"Oh, c'mon," Henry snorted. "And how would that work? I just grab a handful of dirt and shove it in my mouth?"

"Easy as it sounds," said Bastian.

Henry bent over and scooped up some dirt with a disgusted face; he poked out his tongue and tasted the soil.

After a few seconds of chewing it, he said in surprise, "It's delicious." He thrust the whole pile into his mouth. "It tastes like … chocolate."

"We told you so," Bastian said. "Keep eating because you need to recover. Perseverance and determination will give you strength."

Henry was beginning to like being a wizard. He laid down after swallowing the soil and rested for a while. In his mind, it sparked the thought he could really use magic for his benefit.

"Okay, I'm ready," Henry said, standing up. "What do I do now?"

Bastian looked at the documents he had. Henry peered over the other wizard's shoulder at the nonsensical symbols and figures.

"What are these? What does it mean?" he asked.

Bastian said, "These here are magical instruments. Each one gives a certain power. Your horn is one of the most powerful, and there is a lot of energy behind it."

Henry took out his horn and examined it closely.

Bastian continued, "as for the symbols, they are secret spells used along with the instruments; some of the symbols are still unknown."

"I've seen similar images," Henry confessed to Bastian. "My brother has a page from a Veneficum book that looks like this."

"Where did your brother get that page?" asked Bastian.

"In the castle's library, there is an old wooden box locked inside a crystal case. When Tallye gave us the tour in the library, she mentioned that no one's ever opened the crystal, but my brother told me later there is a book inside the wooden box."

"Well then, how does your brother have it?" Bastian asked.

"He opened it with my horn."

Bastian mused, looking concerned. "Did he tell you what the book looked like?"

"He said the cover had a tilted sword, a crossing spear, with two horns and two gauntlet wristbands, all inside a round figure. Like your cloak's symbol."

For a second Bastian's composure shifted. He paced in front of Henry and Nabí, cursing, "Irrumbalus, irrumbalus."

"Why are you freaking out? What's special about that book?" asked Nabí.

"Didn't you teach me how to master myself?" scoffed Henry. "Breathe deeply and relax."

Bastian stopped. "Remiel found a book of his father's that contained powerful spells, symbols, and all the substantial power of the spear, the horns, and the other instruments. You've just described the same book of the One divine. He was the first of the Seven Divine children, the creator of the Strakum Universe and the humans."

"And why did Zadkiel have it?"

"I don't know, but before Remiel pushed me through the portal, he made it disappear so no other wizard or species could use it." He added, "I didn't know the Veneficums had found it."

"Why haven't I ever heard about it?" asked Nabí.

"Besides Remiel's sister, he didn't tell anyone but me. Nobody else knows about the book. He made me promise to keep it a secret and not to look for it," Bastian said. "That's why Tallye didn't pay too much attention to it. I have no clue how they found the book, but this isn't good. They can't discover how to open the crystal case."

Bastian's attention shifted to Henry. "We need to hurry your magic training. By tomorrow, most of the Milaculums will have recovered, and we can rescue Moris by nightfall. Every day it gets more dangerous."

"Finally," said Henry.

"Get stronger with these spells. They'll help you build objects and move them."

He got in position and tried to summon the same power he exhibited earlier, but he failed.

"Now that you've realized it isn't easy, let's try these simple spells. It'll help increase your stamina."

"How can I reach the same energy as before?" Henry asked.

"With patience and practice. When you're more experienced, you may use the trees, but not much, it can become addictive."

"Henry?" Nabí said. "Try again the spell *Utremqua* to create water."

Henry repeated the whole process he'd learned and said, "Utremqua." In that instant, water appeared inside a glass.

"Excellent!" Nabí smiled, and with her freckles, it's like a sudden beam of sunlight.

Henry thought her smile was more awesome than the water.

Bastian said, "Try this spell: Ventul."

Henry shook his shoulders, loosened, and cast the spell. Wind came out of his hand.

"Well done, Henry," Bastian said. "That's it for today. We need to rest, and tomorrow we'll proceed with the strategy."

"I want to help with the rescue," Henry said.

"You're not ready. By tomorrow we'll have sufficient Milaculums recovered, so we can get Moris out. Or do you want us to wait for you to practice more?"

Henry picked up his stuff and said, "We'll go now."

CHAPTER 18
VENEFICUM'S PLANS

Moris started his day with a search for breakfast. As he was about to open the dining-room door, he heard Tallye talking from inside. He put his ears close and listened.

"A strange thing happened yesterday," she said.

"Many strange things have happened since the humans arrived. Now what?" asked Lucio.

"Right after I had dinner with the boy, he got upset about us not rescuing his brother. I sensed a dark force, and the horn started glowing dark green, not dark red. It's the second time this has happened."

Dark force? Wondered Moris.

Lucio paused for a moment. "You said it activated in the boy's hand? Add this to the list of the strange things. I'm sensing that we are heading into the unknown."

"What are we going to do then?" asked Tallye.

"We need to find a way to hold the horn ourselves and use it for dicon. Now that you've found the other horn too, we must get Henry and his horn. The power of the horns needs to be with us. Send someone to the Milaculum's house and see if the human is there—and I mean discreetly. Do you understand?"

"Yes."

"No fights this time. Tell them to report back as soon as they find him."

"Got it," said Tallye, and before she rushed out, Moris hurried outside the castle. He found Glinda on the terrace eating her breakfast and joined her.

"I want a bagel and eggs, please," he said.

Glinda snapped her fingers, and a plate appeared for him. Moris was about to take a bite when Tallye caught up to him. "Hey kid, we need to have a chat."

Moris snorted. "Good morning to you too, Tallye." He finished the bite of food Tallye had interrupted.

Henry's absence was making Moris a different kid.

"What is it now? Are we going for Henry?" Moris asked.

"We're searching for him first ... How are you feeling here?"

Moris frowned. "I'm gonna be honest, I'm scared."

"Yeah, I would feel the same. This is also new for us, and we can't explain it. But I think you've already discovered the horns are special. That's how you could travel here."

"Sounds powerful," Moris said as if he was clueless about it.

"Truth be told, you also activated the horn yesterday. That's why it glowed dark green when you got angry."

"So you noticed?" asked Moris.

"There is something bizarre about it," said Tallye. "The horn only glows for people who have powers. But humans aren't supposed to have powers."

A twin Veneficums came up to them. One of them said in a low voice, "Tallye, you need to come with us."

"What is it? I'm busy with the kid."

The Veneficum mumbled something, hard to hear for Moris.

"Stay here, kid," Tallye said to Moris. She moved away, leaving Moris and Glinda.

Moris watched from the corner of his eye, trying to figure out what they were talking about.

Moments later, she rushed back to Moris and said, "Come."

She grabbed his hand and hauled him back into the castle.

"Where are you taking me? What did they tell you? Is Henry okay?" Moris stammered. They arrived at the Latium Room, where the Veneficums practiced their fighting.

"Wait for me here," she instructed and left Moris alone in the room. He knew something was not right. The last time he was in the Latium room, the Veneficums had compelled him to tell the truth. In the silence of the room, Moris heard shouting just outside. Curious, he headed towards the door. Lucio and Tallye almost bowled him over as they entered. "Boy, you want our help, right?" asked Lucio as he approached.

"Yes, of course. I have to get back to my brother."

"Okay. We need to learn what's going on with you two— who you really are, how you got here, and how we can get you both back to Earth. But we need you to cooperate," Lucio said.

"How can I help?"

"I want to go inside your mind to see what you experienced, so we can figure out how to send you back to Strakum. Can you help me to help you?"

Moris froze, terrified at what that might mean. He didn't want anyone inside his head, but he wanted to go back and be with his mother and Maya.

"I guess so," Moris said, his voice quavering.

With his magic, Lucio moved a chair to the center of the fighting space. "Sit here."

Lucio approached Moris from behind and, with his palm on Moris's head, said, "Animoslu Moriaelus."

Moris's eyes went white. His head trembled. Lucio held on tightly as his eyes also turned white, and he went inside Moris's mind, able to see everything: faces, places, experiences.

The first memory Lucio saw was the woman with the three babies crying. Moris also didn't recognize the babies, but he knew the old lady—the caretaker of the cabin. Lucio went forward in time to when Moris fell off the horse and grabbed the horn, then to when they were playing on the bed and accidentally traveled to Dantus World.

Lucio started to understand. He took Moris's memories further back, before the vacations. It wasn't long he could see Uriel / Moris's Dad / Kevin.

"What the yñak?" Lucio cursed. "This can't be right." He kept watching Moris' memories, and still, it was definitely Uriel. Shocked, he extracted himself from Moris's memories. His eyes returned to normal, and he cast a spell to put Moris semi-unconscious as if drugged.

Lucio kept cursing, "Irrambulus, irrambulus." He paced back and forth.

Without strength to move more, Moris cracked open his eyes to see what was going on.

"What's that matter?" Tallye asked.

"The damn list of strange things keeps getting longer." Lucio kept pacing, trying to process what he'd seen.

"Does it beat Henry doing magic?" asked Tallye.

"The human's father is Uriel."

What? Moris struggled to frown.

"The one who escaped with Miranda and the spear?" Tallye added, "I'm surprised he ended up having human children."

"After he and Miranda took off with the spear, we never found where they were hiding," Lucio said. "The strange thing is that I didn't see her with him. And the humans said their father had vanished, meaning Uriel's also in the window again."

"Then what are we going to do with the boy? Is he a wizard?"

Lucio shrugged. "We need to do the test." He produced a knife out of the air and pricked Moris's arm to draw blood.

Moris groaned.

With his magic, Lucio filled a bowl with water and placed the blood in it to perform the test.

After a few seconds, the water turned green.

"No," shrieked Lucio, flinging the bowl to the wall.

Iggy rushed in through the door. "What's the matter?"

"Iggy! How can the humans be divine?" Lucio shouted.

"What?" Iggy asked, closing the door.

"Long story short, we found Uriel."

Iggy frowned.

Lucio continued, "The humans are not even humans at all. They're divines, Zadkiel descendants."

Moris recalled Zadkiel was the founder of the wizards, but he didn't understand what that meant. He had a lot of questions.

"What are you saying, then?" asked Iggy. "They came from Strakum World. How's that possible?"

"I'm a hundred percent sure. The test confirmed it. And they think Uriel is their father, although they don't know him by that name. The odd thing is that Miranda wasn't there, and Uriel is not a divine family member. Or is he?"

Iggy hesitated. "No, he's not … even if their father is Uriel, how can they be divine?"

"I've no idea how it's possible, but it's true," Lucio said. "Thinking about it, that's why they could travel, hold the horn, and that's why it glowed when the kid got angry."

"What color?" asked Iggy.

"Dark green instead of dark red."

"You didn't tell me that before; that's important, and now I know what to do." Iggy walked over and stood beside Moris. "Here's the deal. The kid has Ivar's horn—you realize what that means. Let's take advantage of that. We'll erase this talk from his memory, only tell him he's capable of magic, and teach him. The horn will turn him evil. But first, you need to unblock the wizard inside him. Free his powers."

Moris struggled to move, but the lethargy spell held him

still. He didn't want to lose his memory.

"What do you mean?" asked Lucio.

"A long time ago, I read that when a wizard's powers are blocked, his energy becomes green."

"The spell 'Abnemlus Montalum' will unblock his powers," Iggy said. "The Milaculums must have known the humans are not really humans. We need to train the boy to our side before the Milaculums come for him."

Iggy turned to leave, but then Lucio said, "One last thing, should we contact Huglan?"

Iggy hesitated. "Now is the right moment."

Lucio commanded Tallye to leave the room. He and Iggy closed their eyes and breathed deeply.

They entered the meditation state, and, in a matter of seconds, a skinny old man, dressed in a long black trench coat, appeared as a soul in the room.

"What the—" Moris mumbled as his head rocked.

"Huglan?" Iggy called.

"Iggy, is that you?" the man said.

"Yeah, and Lucio is here with me."

"Why did you summon me? What's going on? Are we progressing with dicon?"

"We passed the first stage. It worked. When we use another wizard as a conduit, we don't become addicted."

Huglan paused. "But Dantus is still the only Universe where it works."

"We are moving forward to the second stage," said Lucio.

"You need to accelerate things. Other divines are trying to stop us, and we need all the energy we can get."

"That's why we're here," Iggy said. "Some humans arrived at Dantus a few weeks ago, but we just learned they are Zadkiel's descendants. Here is one." Iggy gestured to Moris.

Huglan turned to him and chuckled. "And I'm here in Strakum World looking for them."

"What? You knew there were Zadkiel's descendants and never told us? You said you were looking for the instruments," said Iggy.

"Never question a divine," said Huglan. "Do they have the instruments?"

"Just the horns," replied Lucio.

"You know what to do, right?"

"The kid has the horn you altered. But the other human and horn are with Bastian."

"Get them. Let the kid's horn darken his heart. I'm coming to Dantus."

Iggy asked, "What if we need to summon you again? Does Janka have her energy open to us?"

"I'll tell her to do so," said Huglan. "You better get the other horn before I arrive."

Huglan vanished in the air.

Iggy approached Moris with a bottle. She grasped his hair and pulled his head back until his mouth opened. The liquid she poured down his throat made him cough.

***

Moris woke up in the chair. He groaned, rubbing the cut on his arm. "What happened?" he asked. He didn't remember having any cuts before.

"We found out how you got here," said Lucio. "And you can, in fact, do magic with the horn. We'll teach you how, so you can travel back for yourself. But first, I need to do a spell."

"Awesome!" Moris said.

"That's it? Awesome? Aren't you more curious about it?" asked Tallye.

"I already guessed I could do magic with the horn."

"Take out your horn," said Lucio.

Moris held his horn out.

"Boy! Your life is going to change forever. You'll go through something magical." Lucio put his palm on Moris head and said, "Abnemlus Montalum!"

Although he didn't know it at the time, the same thing happened to Moris that happened to Henry. Blue and green lightning emerged around the horn, and Moris's fingers curled hard around it. He shuddered as lightning traveled from the horn into his body. His body hovered, and his eyes turned completely white. Moris cried out, excited. Then, his body returned to normal and landed softly on the ground.

"That was a rush," Moris said, his voice joyful.

"Now you are ready," Lucio said. "Repeat whatever you did when you sensed the energy in your body."

Moris stood up, shook his arms, and attempted to repeat the same procedure—but failed. He tried again, making gestures, and failed again.

"When I did the magic before, I was angry. I'm trying the same thing, but how can I get angry when I feel great?"

Lucio said wryly, "Let me help you with that."

Lucio approached Moris and performed a spell that forced him into negative memories. Moris recalled the awful ones he'd blocked from his mind, and as they came back, he grew furious. Dark energy sparkled through his body into the horn, and it glowed dark red instead of dark green.

With that energy, Moris said, "Ray."

A small lightning bolt released from the horn.

"Incredible," he breathed. In this particular moment, Moris realized what he could be. For the first time, his dream became a reality. He'd done it on its own, no special Doncelust suit required.

"That's good, kid," Lucio encouraged. "But we're going to teach you the proper spells to reach your full potential. Try again, but this time say, Fulmilum."

Moris repeated the process and said, "Fulmilum!" This time dark red sparks surrounded the horn. Moris's eyes gleamed red, and the horn fired lightning.

"Excellent," Lucio said, grinning darkly. "You need to sense the energy in your body from your emotions and let your horn increase that force."

Moris learned anger was the only way to gain that energy. Lucio gave him some more spells to practice. Each time, Moris got angry, and the red horn gleamed darker and darker, making him a better wizard.

While it corrupted his spirit.

Lucio was pleased at Moris's improvement and said so. Then he announced, "At this rate, you'll get back home sooner than we thought. You won't need the other horn to travel through dimensions."

Moris hesitated. "Are you saying I can travel through worlds with this horn?"

"Oh kid, a whole new world has come to you. With the horn's power, you can achieve the unimaginable. You'll be able to open portals and explore whatever worlds you want."

"That's amazing. When will I be able to do that?"

"Up to you. With your brother, you can go back now if you use both horns—or you can stay and practice until you can do it by yourself whenever you want. What's your choice, kid?"

Moris thought this over. "Henry can wait. He's not in danger, right?" The wicked horn had already warped his mind a little.

"You both are safe on Dantus."

"I want to be with my brother and tell him about this. He could learn to do magic with me. He'll love it."

"I heard he's already practicing magic," Lucio confessed.

Moris made a face. "How do you know?"

"Someone saw him. Maybe that's why he hasn't come for you?"

"I don't believe you."

"Let me show you."

Lucio sent Tallye to bring in the twins. When they arrived, he used a spell to project on the wall what the twins had witnessed: Henry held the horn, and with it appeared a glass of water; he then cast a spell, and wind came out of his hand.

Moris's horn glowed intensely dark red as he watched the images. His brother seemed happy and he felt abandoned.

He yelled, "Aahh! Ventrulum!"

He fired out a windstorm, blowing Lucio and Tallye away to land on the ground some distance away.

"Unbelievable," Lucio said as he got up, cleaning his pants. He looked at Tallye with a malicious smile and winked. Ivar's horn was doing its job.

"How come my brother is practicing magic instead of trying to be with me?"

"I don't know. But if you learn to use the horn, you can go back home without him."

"Keep teaching me then." Moris felt a strange sensation of magic in his blood.

"I will, but it's time to take a break. I don't know about you, but I'm hungry." Lucio led them to the dining room.

At dinner, Lucio asked, "Moris, how strong do you want to be?"

"What do you mean?"

"Well, you can practice simple spells for fun, or you can be powerful and do extraordinary things."

"I want to be powerful."

"Yes, indeed. I have some spells for you to practice."

"Awesome." Moris grinned from ear to ear. He was finally starting to like Lucio and Tallye.

Then he turned to her and asked, "Why is your sister on the other side fighting against you?"

Tallye groaned. "I once was with the Milaculums, and Nabí and I were inseparable. When our parents died, she became my rock. We did everything together. They called us Tanna, which means beloved sisters. But then I started to hear wizards saying that Nabí was the smartest, the better wizard. That I'm nothing without her. I became her shadow, making me feel less. One day we were practicing magic, and she beat me as always. So I ran away to cry alone. That's when Lucio came to me and promised that I would become powerful and greater than my sister. I just needed to join the Veneficums and practice their kind of magic. I'll never go back."

"Do you miss her?" Moris asked.

Tallye's face grew wistful. Before she answered, Lucio jumped in and said, "Did you know your horn is special? It's stronger than your brother's. You can use it by itself, or all three together."

"There's a third?"

"The third piece is a spear."

Lucio began a long-winded explanation about the seven instruments and their powers. Moris tuned it out, wondering who was actually on his side. *The Veneficums haven't done anything bad to me, but still sometimes they seem rude. And Vinghy … she seems nice. But why did they take my brother?*

Sitting at the dining table, Lucio held out his hand, and papers hovered towards him from across the room. He gave them to Moris. "Practice these spells with your horn. The more you practice, the stronger you'll get. Soon you won't even need the horn."

CHAPTER 19
THE REUNION

It was getting late, and after a day of practicing complex spells, Moris was tired. He headed to his room and laid down. He closed his eyes and tried to sleep, but his mind was hungry for more magic. He couldn't avoid it, so he opened his eyes and cast a spell. This time his whole vision turned red. He uttered another spell and felt a strange dark energy within him.

Out of nowhere, an explosion boomed outside and the castle fell into blackness. The flaming torches died, the sky turned red. Birds entered the room, flying everywhere in a frenzy. Veneficums scrambled around outside the castle. Their tigers sprang through the yard, roaring and running wild. The owls whirled insanely. Deer fought each other, fish jumped out of the river, and all the animals in the forest acted crazy.

The horn compelled Moris to continue using it, so he sat on the bed practicing his spells. His eyes turned red, and he went into a trance.

Out of the chaos, Vinghy forced the door open and

entered. She stood paralyzed for a moment. "Moris?" she asked in a puzzled voice.

He didn't move or blink. He stayed hypnotized, casting minor spells to hover the potion and make sparks in the air. The horn blinked an intense dark red.

"Uh-oh," she mumbled and went to Moris. His mind was struggling, fighting the unknown force.

Vinghy snapped, "Moris!"

Moris didn't react. Not even a blink.

Vinghy tried again. But this time, she slapped his face. "Moris?"

Moris jerked and dropped his horn. "Wha—Vinghy? What are you doing here?"

"We agreed to meet in the Gonlu Room. What happened?"

"Nothing? I didn't see any signal."

"How could you miss it? Did you look outside?"

"How did you get out?" Moris asked.

"Me? How did you get out of the Mortus Door? It doesn't matter now. It's time to get out of here and find your brother—quickly now."

"Let me grab the horn."

Vinghy took Moris by the hand, and they began sneaking out in the darkness.

A Veneficum loomed out of the darkness and bumped into them. Unable to see them, he demanded, "Who are you?"

"We're heading downstairs, like everyone else," said Vinghy.

The Veneficum lit up a torch from the wall and lifted it up to see them. "Wait."

Vinghy stopped, whispering to Moris, "Don't turn around."

"I'm coming with you," said the Veneficum.

He got closer, and the light of the torch revealed Vinghy's face. She turned away to hide her face, but that only aroused his suspicions. He peered closer at them.

His eyes widened in recognition. Vinghy gave him no time to react further. She punched the Veneficum right on the nose, knocking him out, then grabbed the falling body so it wouldn't thud on the floor.

"Quickly, keep going," said Vinghy.

Arriving at the Gonlu Room, they ducked down the hallway leading to the kitchen. Another Veneficum came running past and Vinghy stood back, pulling Moris back, so he didn't discover them. The Veneficum passed them without noticing.

"That was close," said Moris.

Vinghy peeked down the hallway cautiously. It was empty. "Okay, let's go."

They made it to the kitchen, only to bump into another Veneficum. This one was faster and immediately hovered kitchen knives and fired them at Vinghy. Vinghy released Moris and blocked them.

"Hide, Moris," said Vinghy.

The Veneficum blasted an electric ball and Vinghy counterattacked with lightning. Next, the Veneficum lunged to grab Moris. Vinghy flipped over the table and tossed a wind at the Veneficum. The Veneficum snarled. He shook his fist and a flame appeared on it.

Moris ducked under the table.

The Veneficum went for Vinghy and threw a punch of fire. She dodged his fist, and her eyes followed the flame before her as if it was in slow motion. Her elbow smote into his chest and crawled him back. The Veneficum touched his chest, moaning, and then hovered all the knives around Vinghy.

Moris got desperate and came out under the table. He clutched his horn, and without hesitating, he called, "Ventul!"

The windstorm he made took Vinghy and the Veneficum by surprise. It blew them both back, along with the remains of the kitchen.

"What the heck was that?" grunted Vinghy as she got up.

She glanced around at the mess, then limped towards the Veneficum, who lay on the floor groaning in pain. She cast "Somnulum," putting him to sleep.

They got out to the backyard, heading to the castle wall. They almost made it to the wall when a voice said, "Where are you taking the kid, Vinghy?"

They stopped and turned around. Lucio stood with a band of Veneficums at his back. The battle in the kitchen must have alerted them.

"Damn it," said Vinghy. It was pointless to fight; they outnumbered her. "He's leaving with me," she said to Lucio.

"Ah, okay," Lucio chuckled. "You think we're just going to let you leave? Besides, he wants to stay to practice magic. Isn't that right, kid?"

Moris looked at Vinghy, who frowned. He asked himself

what to do. The feeling he sensed for magic was appealing, but he also wanted to be with Henry.

Vinghy lowered her head. "Moris? Your brother is looking for you, and you can practice magic with us. They only want your horn."

"Bring me the human," Lucio commanded to his Veneficums.

The Veneficums form in position, ready to fight.

Vinghy stepped in front of Moris.

The Veneficums, all at once, cast a spell and attacked.

Vinghy watched as fire, lightning, wind and water bolts headed towards her. She closed her eyes and prepared to block all the attacks.

Out of nowhere, a colossal shield came down in front of them.

Vinghy opened her eyes and gasped in relief. On top of the castle wall stood Bastian with the other Milaculums, jumping into the castle.

"Hurry, the shield won't last long. Run," shouted Bastian.

Vinghy turned to Moris and said, "Trust me about what I'm going to do." She took Moris's horn and flung it away. As it fell, she cast a spell to grow vines from the ground to entangle it permanently. She then grabbed Moris's hand and ran away with him.

"No! What are you doing? That's my horn! Let me go!"

Vinghy cast a spell to put him semi-unconscious, the same one Lucio had cast earlier. He felt her pick up his body and start running.

Lucio and the Veneficums went after Vinghy and Moris,

but the shield stopped them.

Tallye arrived to help Lucio. "What do we do?" she asked.

"Leave them; we have the horn. By the time we break the shield, they'll be gone."

CHAPTER 20
THE MORTUS DOOR MYSTERY

The Milaculums arrived at their house with Moris, now unconscious.

"Oh! Thank god," Henry said with a big smile. "Thank you very much, Vinghy. You took such a risk to save my brother."

"You know who I am?" she asked.

"They told me about you, Vinghy the Mighty. I'm Henry, Moris's brother." Henry held out his hand. When she reached out to meet him, he saw her crystal ring.

He said, "Nice ring. Does it mean something?"

"I can tell you it is millions of years old and has passed through thousands of generations."

"Ah. Again, thank you so much."

"Let me wake him up. He was angry when I put him to sleep. You might want to step back."

Henry and the Milaculums moved away as Vinghy laid Moris on the ground. She cast the spell to awaken him. He opened his eyes and lunged at Vinghy.

"Where is my horn?" Moris snarled as he fought to reach Vinghy.

"Relax, Moris. We're back together now." Henry gave Moris a hug to calm him down. "I missed you."

Moris looked at his brother. A moment passed, then a smile came, and he hugged back. "I missed you too, Henry."

Nabí asked, "What did Moris mean about his horn?"

Vinghy explained, then said, "But don't worry, Moris. Look in your pocket."

Moris put his hand to his pocket. He felt something and took it out—there was the horn, intact.

"I never took the horn," said Vinghy.

"How did it get here?" Moris asked.

"It was an illusion for Lucio. You always had the real horn."

Moris gazed at the horn, and immediately it glowed dark red.

Vinghy and Bastian looked at each other. The horn shone red instead of green, meaning they'd unblocked Moris' powers.

Moris turned to Henry, who seemed happy to see him. "I thought you weren't coming for me."

"Are you kidding? Every day I wanted to come for you. How could you think otherwise?"

"Lucio said you were doing your own magic, and that's why you didn't come for me."

Henry, Bastian, and Nabí glanced at each other, followed by a moment of silence.

"That's crazy. I'd never leave you behind," said Henry.

"Is it true that you are practicing magic?" Moris asked.

"That's true, Moris," Henry said quietly. "But my powers are limited, so that's why I didn't go with Bastian and the others to the castle. They thought it was too dangerous."

Milaculums started whispering among themselves. The humans weren't supposed to be able to do magic.

"How do you know about Henry?" Bastian asked.

"A Veneficum saw him practicing outside somewhere," Moris said.

"The Epiculus Forest, that's not good," Bastian said.

The Milaculums kept looking at each other until one of them asked, "What's going on, Bastian? What haven't you told us about these humans?"

Bastian hesitated and sighed. "Milaculums, truth be told, they are not humans at all. They are Zadkiel's descendants."

A harsh gasp from each of the Milaculums.

Bastian continued, "Ominous times are ahead. Veneficums will try to get the horns from us. Prepare yourselves."

"Prepare for what?" Henry asked as the Milaculums murmured amongst themselves.

"For the battle over control of the horns. The Veneficums know who you really are."

Moris flinched. "Me?"

Bastian chuckled. "Don't try to look surprised. I know."

"How?" Moris asked.

"I saw your horn glow when you grabbed it. That means you've been practicing magic." Bastian added, "Be careful with that horn. Don't practice with it, it's wicked and corrupts the one who uses it."

"Is it true, Moris? You too practiced magic?" Henry asked.

Vinghy said, "Yes. But then, you also need to explain how you got out the Mortus Door."

Henry said, alarmed, "You entered the Mortus Door? I told you never to do that. How did you get out?"

"Vinghy, what are you talking about?" said Moris. "I didn't enter the Mortus Door."

"I saw you while I was meditating, then you disappeared."

"That's not true. I never entered the door."

Bastian went to Moris and said grimly, "Moris, no one knows what's behind the Mortus Door. Did you really enter the door?"

"No … or at least, I don't remember."

"I saw you," Vinghy said.

Everyone looked at Moris.

Moris felt the weight of their gazes on him. "You can do the spell to look into my mind," he was compelled to respond.

"I trust you both," said Bastian. "But I would like to see for myself."

Bastian put his hand above Moris and did the spell to see inside his mind. He saw what Moris experienced during his stay with the Veneficums and how the Veneficums used the addicted wizards. Bastian gasped in horror and surprise.

"Those are Collolums. How dare they?"

Moris said, "They are helping those wizards because they're addicted and will die if they don't renew their energy."

Bastian snorted. "Who do you think got them addicted?

They're taking advantage of them to increase their power. I'd never have guessed they were capable of sinking so low."

Bastian continued through Moris's memories and until he saw the two-headed beast in the woods. "Who is that? How could he hold your horn?"

Moris shrugged. "I wondered the same thing; the horn did nothing to him. And he's not a beast; Tallye said he's a cursed Manzokan who escaped from his people when they arrived a few weeks ago. He terrified me at first, but he was gentle and saved me from a Veneficum."

"A Manzokan? It's strange I didn't hear about their arrival." Bastian looked at Vinghy. "Is he from your Universe?"

Vinghy smiled, staying silent.

"You haven't told me where you're from … Find out why the Manzokans were here. And find this cursed Manzokan."

Moris remembered one more thing. "He said the words 'Manjura Tanjara Myla', do you know what that means?"

Bastian hesitated and said, "No. That's up to you to discover."

Bastian moved forward through the memories, but all of a sudden, he was blocked and couldn't go further. He pressed again on the memory, but there was nothing more—as if that part of Moris's memory was erased.

After several attempts, Bastian said, "There's a memory block on your mind; that's why you can't remember. I can't remove it."

"What?" Moris asked. "Who would block my memory? And why? What if they erased something else?"

"I got something," Bastian said as he found the moment

where Iggy erased Moris's memory. He unblocked that experience and watched it.

"Huglan," muttered Bastian but then stayed silent and worried.

Vinghy said, "I saw Moris inside the room. Did Moris travel to the … no, it can't be. He's just a kid. But then, he survived."

"Explain your thoughts, Vinghy," said Bastian.

"Moris soul might've traveled to the eternity dimension or to a lost city," Vinghy said.

"What are you talking about?" asked Henry.

Vinghy explained, "A lost city is a place that moves through Universes and appears from time to time. That's where you found the horns. And the eternity dimension … never mind, that's too complicated to get into. I'll let you know when I find out more."

Henry furrowed his brow. "Did you practice magic, Moris?" He asked again.

Moris paused, humming. "Yes, it's true. They taught me magic spells when they found out about you."

"Did they train you?" asked Henry.

"I don't think so," replied Bastian. "Ivar's horn is easier to use and doesn't exhaust the one who uses it because Huglan altered it. It isn't like Remiel's horn."

"Do they know we are divine?" Henry asked.

"Yes, they know," Bastian said. "They did the test on him, and now they also know that your father is Uriel."

"Uriel? Divine? What are you talking about?" Moris demanded, bewildered.

"Moris, they've been hiding the truth from you," said Bastian.

"Yeah," said Moris, his voice slow. "Lucio said my life will change forever when he did the spell to give me powers."

Bastian explained about the Seven Divine and the children of the Divine Zadkiel and his wife Andela: Miranda, Ivar, and Remiel, and what happened to them. He described what little he knew about the powerful instruments, especially Moris's horn. Then added, "The Seven Divine each ruled their own Universe, and each had a particular instrument that was very powerful…"

Bastian also told him about the fake potion Moris had been drinking and who his father was: Uriel The Omnimus, the greatest Milaculum who ever existed.

Moris gawked, hearing all this.

Bastian created some magic water and said, "Drink this."

Moris didn't hear him, his mind was lost in thought about what he might be able to accomplish with magic powers. *I could fly, teleport, and tease Maya.*

"*Moris*," Bastian said.

Moris jerked. "What?"

"Drink this. This water will counteract the Veneficums' potion, so you won't suffer like your brother did when the potion faded away."

Moris frowned. He turned to Henry, and Henry nodded.

He drank it.

CHAPTER 21
ONE'S DESIRE ARE NOT EVERYONE'S DESIRES

A stormy mood hung over the Milaculum's house. Sooner or later, the Veneficums would come raiding.

"Milaculums, gather around," Bastian shouted to all the wizards in the house. "Now you know we have the two horns and these two humans — divines — who came from Strakum. That said, you can expect a coming fight with the Veneficums. Whatever happens, we protect our homes. Don't let them take the humans and the horns. The time has arrived for the Veneficums to vanish from Dantus."

"How can we help?" Henry asked.

"Keep a hold of the horn and don't get caught by Lucio," Bastian replied.

The Milaculums used their powers to build an enormous shield around the house. They laid traps outside and set in a store of magical objects and poisons.

A Milaculum came out running from the front gate.

"Bastian! Bastian! The Veneficums are coming."

"How far out are they?" asked Bastian calmly.

"An hour away."

"That fast?" Another wizard asked, his voice surprised.

"They are in a hurry for the horns. Prepare yourself," yelled Bastian.

The Milaculums went into an uproar and ran toward their assigned positions.

Henry and Moris spun, clueless about what to do.

Some Milaculums stayed outside the house. The Veneficums would come with their entire arsenal because they didn't yet have the horns or the humans. They did, however, have more wizards and animal-beasts.

"Henry, Moris, come," said Bastian as he pulled them inside the house.

Henry struggled with his new feelings. *Should I stay and fight with them or leave once and for all?* He'd fallen for Nabí's beauty and his friendship with Bastian. Then he thought of his mother and Maya.

"Bastian, we need to go back home," Henry said

"We can fight with them, Henry. We have powers," Moris said enthusiastically.

Bastian said, "It's perilous to use Ivar's horn, Moris. It will change your soul."

"But Vinghy promised you'd teach me."

Bastian hesitated. "I'll teach you another time," he said. "You don't know what you're getting into if you use that horn. It's extremely dangerous."

Henry said, "We need to go home now, Moris. Think

about Mom and Maya; they must be worried sick. We can practice our magic on Earth." Henry knew that wouldn't happen. Once they arrived on Earth, he'd get rid of the horns.

Moris groaned.

"It's better for all of us if you leave," Bastian said. "Take the horns. To open the portal, you need both horns together and a spell—"

The house quaked from an explosion outside. It sent Bastian and the brothers staggering. The Veneficums and their beasts had attacked with an explosive flame.

"Prepare for battle!" Bastian yelled through the door at the Milaculums standing outside. The Milaculums released their animal fighters, the Ouglus, and Ragus. The Ouglus looked like Earth eagles and the Ragus like Earth dingos, but grey with brown eyes.

"Really? Are these their animal fighters?" mumbled Moris.

The Veneficums surrounded the fortress with their tiger and owl creatures. They stopped before the shield. An awkward silence fell between the two sides as they waited for their respective commands to attack.

Lucio turned to both sides, looking at his Veneficums, and yelled, "Attack!"

The Veneficums and their wild animals attacked by slamming themselves against the shield. Inside, Bastian and the Milaculums were waiting, watching how the shield held. They knew eventually it would break.

By the time the shield broke, the Milaculums stood in defensive formation.

Lucio shouted, "Charge!"

The Veneficums, including their beasts, took off after the Milaculums. As they advanced, their feet began to stick to the ground.

Hands sprouted up from the liquid and held the Veneficum's legs. Lucio and a few superior Veneficums released themselves with magic, but the rest struggled.

Bastian headed out of the house with the rest of the Milaculums who stood in line waiting for the Veneficums. Henry and Moris followed.

Bastian walked in front of the line, turned to his wizards, and shouted, "Milaculums! You know what will happen to our world and to the Universes if they succeed. Fight as if there was no tomorrow—neither the horns nor the humans can be taken." He watched the Veneficums struggling with the liquid for a moment, then continued, "The existence of all the Universes is on us. Charge!"

The Milaculums howled and attacked together as they rushed the entrapped Veneficums.

Vinghy lifted her arm and cast a spell. Rocks from the ground hovered, gathered, and formed into several rock-balls surrounded with blue fire. With great force, she hurled it towards the Veneficums.

Bastian lifted sticks and wood from the ground and brought them together, forming sharp spears with lightning.

The Milaculum dingos transformed into a large, light brown furry lion-dingo with sharp fangs and pointed jaws, their eyes changing to blue.

The dingos galloped towards the tigers. They opened

their muzzles, and a poison trickled down their fangs. As they roared, they released it and melted the tigers, who were stuck in the liquid.

"That's what I'm talking about," Moris cried.

The Veneficums threw spells at the sticky liquid, desperately trying to get free and to defend themselves at the same time.

Lucio and Iggy hovered over them.

Lucio watched his Veneficums struggling to defend themselves or move. "This is not good!" he said.

"You help those," Iggy said, pointing to the left. "And I'll help this side."

Little by little, they began to get rid of the spell. Once they were free to counterattack, Iggy yelled, "Advance."

Bastian turned, and his face dropped as the now free legion of wizards started striking the Milaculums from all sides. Bastian built a shield, but his magic alone wasn't enough. Milaculums got injured, some others vanished.

The battle continued, and the Veneficums surrounded Bastian and the Milaculums. In the clash, the jail where the Milaculums imprisoned Galio and other Veneficums broke open, and they also joined the clash.

Bastian watched the Milaculums losing the battle. It was only a matter of time for them, as in when he fought the New Beginning Battle. He followed what his mentor Remiel would do. *The horns and the humans need to leave now.* He dashed to the humans who were outside the house, watching everything.

"Get inside the house," said Bastian.

"But we can fight," Moris replied.

"Don't be silly." Henry took his brother by the shoulder

and as they turned, Moris sensed an energy approaching them.

The boy whirled around and spelled, "Practelus!" He blocked a bolt of lightning, then fired a windstorm at the Veneficum who attacked them.

"Geez," Henry cried.

"I told you, we can help. I just saved you," said Moris, as the horn glowed dark red.

Bastian gaped. "He really can help us," he said. But then he looked at the evil horn's glow. "If you really want to help, go inside and don't use your horn."

"No," Moris snarled. His eyes reddened with magic.

Henry held his brother's shoulders. "Moris, look at me. We are no experts on magic powers. Mom and Maya want us alive."

"You're right," he replied in a low voice as his eyes returned to normal. "I want to practice magic but, at the same time, I really wanted to go back home and see them."

"Let's go home, Moris."

The brothers hurried toward the house. Before they got there, Glinda and three other Veneficums came and snatched Moris from behind.

Henry turned. "Moris!"

Bastian halted Henry. "No. You can't. It's dangerous." He called, "Vinghy," and gestured towards the retreating Veneficums and Moris. "Save the kid."

Vinghy nodded and dashed after them.

***

The Veneficums dragged Moris into the forest. When they stopped to rest, the one who had Moris said, "let's kill the boy and take the horn. We'll tell Lucio he died in battle."

"Yes," those around him agreed.

Moris shuddered. He glanced at Glinda. His face fell at her lack of response. He took out the horn to defend himself, but the Veneficum stopped him.

Blue electricity sparked and massed in the Veneficum's hand. Moris's heart pounded—death was upon him.

With the electric field in Veneficum's hand, the wizard hurled a bolt.

"*No*," Glinda shrieked, throwing herself in front of Moris to block the lightning. "We are not killing the boy," she said as she pushed the Veneficum.

Moris was surprised. He wondered why she'd saved him.

"Why not? We can take the horn."

"Because—" She hesitated. "He's divine; we need him."

"No, we don't. We just need the horn."

"I said no," shouted Glinda and hurled the Veneficum away with dust. "We'll take him to Lucio. He needs the boy to continue with the dicon."

Right then, someone came from the sky and thumped at the Veneficum. It was Vinghy.

Glinda and the others turned.

"Attack," said Glinda.

The Veneficums lashed out. Vinghy zigzagged through the lightning bolts, flame, and spears they hurled at her. She somersaulted and smote a Veneficum in the belly. Spinning to the one beside, she grabbed him by his head and flung him at a tree.

Now it was only Vinghy and Glinda.

Vinghy paced towards Glinda. The sound of approaching Veneficums halted her. She hurried back to Moris and placed him behind her.

Quavering, Moris asked, "What are we going to do?"

"Stay put and close your eyes."

Moris obeyed. With his eyes closed, he felt rather than see a great wind blowing. Peeking, he saw Vinghy spinning like an out-of-control top.

The wind blew harder as she spun faster. Soon, a protective dust tornado formed around them. It burned the Veneficums as they tried to get close. Vinghy stopped spinning and embraced Moris tightly. Shining white wings came out of her before leaping high into the sky and hovering off the battlefield.

"Awesome," he said with a smile plastered on his face. At least until he looked down. Below them, wizards were fighting each other, and beasts were hunting people. It was an awful sight.

Vinghy hid her wings and hovered Moris down back to the Milaculum house.

"Moris!" said Henry, running to him. Bastian followed to protect them.

The brothers hugged each other tightly, Henry still shaking.

"Henry, I flew," Moris said.

Henry chuckled. "After everything, you still are excited."

He ruffled Moris' hair. "C'mon, let's get inside."

The brothers went inside the house and watched the battle from the safety of the window.

In the sky, the Milaculum eagles emerged with sharp claws and beaks and fought the owls and their spiky talons. An owl spread his wings and as he fluttered, daggers launched, cutting an eagle. The owl tried the same move again, but the eagle flapped its wings, causing a windstorm to blow away the blades. The eagle flew upward to the owl, wedged its claws into the owl's head, then spun rapidly as the owl struggled to extricate itself. The eagle flew as high as it could and, with a spin, heaved the owl towards the ground.

"Awesome. Did you see that, Henry?" Moris asked, thrilled with the fighting.

To the left, Nabí was fighting her sister Tallye. They threw all kinds of power at each other. Tallye made sharp crystals appear in the air. Nabí cast a spell and blasted them.

"Stop, Tallye," Nabí shrieked. "I don't want to fight you."

Tallye groaned and continued the attacks. Hers were stronger, but Nabí was the smarter fighter. Tallye made a spell of tree branches—Nabí used a hologram to throw Tallye off and make her miss, but not for long. The tree branch whipped around and grabbed Nabí by her foot and yanked her down.

Exhausted and gasping for air, Nabí said, quavering, "Sister, please."

Tallye glowered and fired an electric windstorm, whirling Nabí through the air until she fell to the ground. With no energy at all, Nabí knelt and panted wearily.

Tallye said, "It's time I prove to everyone who's better." She began pulling energy to her body. She mumbled spells, and her fist gleamed, brighter and brighter, then she shouted, "Fulgurum!" A potent bolt of lightning discharged from her fist towards her sister.

Nabí lifted her head, saw the lightning coming, and grunted as she rushed to move, but she had no energy left. She closed her eyes and waited for the blast.

It didn't come. Galio was holding off the attack as he was holding the lightning; his cloak turned grey like the Collolums.

"Traitor," Tallye shouted. She pushed the lightning hard against Galio's protection.

"Get up, Nabí. Help me. I can't hold it any longer," Galio said, gasping.

Nabí thrust herself to her feet and, together with Galio pushed the lightning away.

Tallye cried in shock; the lightning was flying towards her. It came quick and struck her in the chest.

"No," Nabí cried and rushed to her. "Tallye? Tallye!"

Tallye groaned in pain.

Nabí came with tears swelling in her eyes. Tallye tried to move her lips, but no words came. She grabbed some strength and muttered, "…sister …"

"C'mon Tallye, please get up."

No response at all.

"No. Don't die. Please don't die," Nabí sobbed as she held her sister's body.

"You … were … the perfect girl," Tallye whispered.

"That's not true. I always wanted your kindness and smile. We were happy together, and you were perfect until you changed. I'm sorry, Tallye, I didn't mean to hurt you." A cascade of tears fell.

"You always …" Tallye gasped, with no energy left.

"No! Don't leave me, sister." Nabí put her head beside Tallye's. Her tears reached Tallye's cheeks.

Tallye took a last deep breath and whispered in Nabí's ear, "Tanna forever …" Her eyes closed, and her corpse disintegrated into sand, meaning her spirit had unfinished business.

Galio approached and said, "I'm sorry, Nabí. It wasn't your fault."

"Wasn't it?" Nabí snapped, snuffling. "I should've tried harder to bring her back, but I left her alone."

"Now is not the time for mourning. They are killing your friends," Galio said.

"Why did you help me?"

"You didn't kill me the last time we met. You pardoned my life when they left me behind to die."

Nabí held her cry. "Thank you, Galio." She looked around at the mess. "The humans might need my help."

She departed.

***

Eventually, Lucio and the Veneficums surrounded Bastian and the Milaculums. There was nowhere to go, and they were outweighed in people and power.

"Stop," yelled Lucio as he floated over the wizards.

For an instant, the battle paused.

"Surrender, Bastian. Give us the horns," Lucio called.

"That's not going to happen," replied Bastian.

"We'll kill everyone and take the horns and the divines, anyway."

Henry and Moris looked at each other. Their eyes widened, frightened.

"They have nothing to do with this world," Bastian said. "Let them go back to Strakum World."

"If they were only humans," Lucio smirked. "Besides, the kid wants to practice magic. He loves it."

"You'll have to go through me," Bastian said.

"Through all of us," Vinghy shouted as all the Milaculums formed in line.

"As you wish," Lucio rasped, still hovering.

At that moment, a song echoed over the hills.

Ameeee heee hoo, Amena … hena … hum
Ameeee heee hoo, Amena … hena … hum
Amena hena hum hum, Amena hena hom …
Amena hena hum hum, Amena hena hom …

"What's that?" Lucio demanded. He glanced around. The trees blocked his vision. "Where's that coming from?" he asked, desperate. The anthem seemed to come from the air itself.

Out of nowhere, a fireball hit Lucio in the back and sent him spinning to the ground. A vast bluish flame came out from the trees, heading toward the battle.

It was the Collolums.

"For Vikthor!" They roared with rage and rushed out from the woods. They attacked from behind. Half of the Veneficums turned and fought back, forcing them to stop surrounding the Milaculums.

Anori, Vikthor's younger sister, came out from the trees and a Veneficum engaged her with a fire spear.

With teary eyes, she outstretched her arm, waited for the spear to come close, and then clenched her fist and destroyed it. She next mumbled a spell, and sparks grew around her entire body. With a twirl, she fired a powerful beam. The Veneficum built a shield to block it, but it came through and blew him away.

"That's for my brother," she shrieked with a lump in her heart.

***

The battle kept going, and it injured a lot of wizards, some of them dying.

Bastian took a look around. The place was destroyed. He saw Nabí and called for her.

"Despite the help of the Collolums, it doesn't look good," he said. "We need to show the humans their way to Strakum World."

They rushed inside the house to where Moris and Henry were hidden.

Bastian said, "Henry, you need to leave now." They followed Bastian to the basement and Bastian pressed a brick of the wall—

a secret tunnel opened. "The spell to go back is Itenelum Strakum. It will open the portal. Do you understand?"

"Yes, Itenelum Strakum and enter the portal ... got it," said Henry, then added, "Why don't we do it right now?"

"They are too close, and the portal doesn't shut right away. We must get far away from them. Nabí will stay here, so no one enters the tunnel. Let's go."

"Wait," yelled Nabí as she reached to grasp Henry's hand. She said, "may we meet again," and kissed Henry on the cheek, then hugged him.

Henry blushed. "It was nice to meet you, Nabí ... Goodbye."

Henry left with Moris and Bastian through the secret passage. It was gloomy and had leaves attached to the wall.

"What was that?" Moris scoffed.

"Nothing, we just became friends," Henry said.

"Just friends? Ha! That kiss says otherwise. Look at your face," Moris said.

"Shut up, Moris."

"You know we can go back another time, right?"

Henry balked. "Yeah ... you want that, right? Maya and Mom need us. Bastian, show us the way."

Bastian moved through the tunnel until there was a gate above them, in the ground. "There it is." He pushed open the door and got out.

Bastian whispered, "I heard something." They all halted.

Henry glanced around and saw three Veneficums patroling.

"There! The humans." The Veneficums rushed at them.

Bastian fired sharp thorns to stall them. More Veneficums were coming.

"You need to go quickly. I'll hold them," Bastian said.

"No, we need to fight." Moris grabbed his horn and yelled, 'Fulmilum!' The horn charged with electricity and Moris's hand trembled. He closed his eyes and sent a thunderbolt towards a Veneficum.

Damn it. He is right, Henry thought. He'd tried to avoid using magic, yet they had no choice but to fight.

Again, Moris cast a spell, and flame came out of his fist; his eyes reddened. "Yeah," he roared and smirked as he burned another Veneficum. Each time, Ivar's horn beamed red.

Bastian and the brothers were surrounded. They gathered close to defend each side. Bastian spelled "Pila Clipuslu", and a bubble shield appeared around them.

The Veneficums attacked.

"Open the shield; I can fight," Moris ordered Bastian as his horn flashed red.

"No. There are too many."

Henry snatched Moris's horn, and the red glow faded from his eyes. Holding both horns, Henry stood in the middle of the shield and closed his eyes. He took several long deep breaths; his mind and heart relaxed, beating at the same rhythm.

"What are you doing? Moris asked.

Henry repeated the process he'd learned from Bastian, and leaves and rocks started to hover. A colored light shone in the sky. The tree branches swayed towards Henry and a light began to gleam in their trunks. The light then moved onto the branches, and an aura came out and headed to Henry. Each horn glowed intensely, dark red and dark blue.

"He is doing it," Bastian said, troubled. At that point, he couldn't stop Henry.

Henry's body vibrated as the energy was drawn to him. Blue-red lightning swirled around him. Electric clouds appeared above, the wind blew stronger, and a tornado formed. It tore trees from the ground. Henry opened his red-gleaming eyes and the tornado intensified. With both horns outstretched, he called, "Ventulum… Petraculus!"

A tremendous explosion surged around them, breaking the shield and flinging away the Veneficums.

Moris gaped. It took him a moment to react after seeing that incredible power. "That was *awesome*."

Henry panted as the red and blue electricity vanished.

Bastian was aghast. "No. You can't use the red horn, and you need to leave now. They're gone, but not for long. The others must've felt the explosion."

"Let's go, Moris," said Henry, gasping and limping.

As they were leaving, Bastian shouted, "Remember, 'Itenelum, Strakum.'"

"Yes," shouted Henry as they ran away.

Soon, the sound of battle faded. Only the footsteps of the brothers echoed. Henry glanced around and nobody was close—only trees.

"Okay, Moris, we're alone here. Here's your horn. Together we say, Itenelum, Strakum."

Moris took the horn from Henry, and immediately

Henry felt a strange sensation passing through his body.

Moris asked, "Don't you want to stay a little longer?"

"No, Moris. Come on. Let's go home." Henry's voice grew more insistent.

"Yeah, but we can go home whenever we want. Did you know that we have the potential to travel to any universe?"

"I told you, we'll practice on Earth," Henry growled in desperation.

Moris frowned. He peered at Henry's horn, and it had Warkru's symbols. Henry had given him the wrong horn.

"Henry, you have my horn, let's switch," Moris said.

"It doesn't matter, Moris!" Henry rasped.

"Okay, you're right," Moris was startled. "Let's say 'Itenelum, Strakum' together with the horns."

Henry was hypnotized like Moris had when he used Ivar's horn for the first time. Henry's eyes glowed red.

"Henry! Itenelum, Strakum."

Henry jerked. "Yeah, right. On the count of three?"

"Yes, one … two … three."

"Itenelum, Strakum!"

A black circle in the sky was surrounded by sparks of blue energy. A portal opened before them.

The horn gleamed intensely dark red, sending dark energy to Henry's body.

"Henry, let's go."

Henry balked. "You go."

"What?"

"I've a strange feeling about magic. I'm going to stay."

"What the heck, Henry? You were right. We need to go

home and be with Mom and Maya," Moris said. "Come on!" he grasped Henry's hand.

Henry snapped, "No! I'll stay!" The horn flashed dark red. "You be with Mom and Maya. I'll be fine."

"But I need you!" cried Moris.

"I'm not your father," yelled Henry, as his eyes turned darker red.

Moris was stunned and bewildered. "What's happened to you?" He looked at the portal as it started to close. "We have to get home before the portal closes."

"I said no! Ventrulum!" Henry spelled with Ivar's horn, pushing his brother with a windstorm to the portal.

"Henry!" Moris screamed. "No!"

The portal closed, and Henry stayed in the Dantus World with Ivar's horn. Its dark energy had a price, and that price was: betraying his loving brother.

EPILOGUE

Henry flung Moris inside a black hole.

"No!" he shouted. Complete blackness as he fell between Universes. Places and people projected in the darkness. A man walking in the middle of two hills. *Who is he?* Moris thought, squinting.

The man turned around.

Moris gasped, and his heart skipped a beat.

"Dad?" he said.

The man frowned, looked up.

Blue energy sparked through the black circle in the sky as a body fell, smashing the ground with a thud. The portal vanished.

Moris rapidly stood up. "No, no, no, — Why? What the hell, Henry? What have you *done*?" he howled, searching for the portal. He paced side to side, hands wringing. *This can't be happening,* he kept thinking. A lump formed in his gut and his breath quickened. The more he thought about it, the more his heart raced. The tension moved through his chest, up his throat, until he unleashed a scream of fury to the sky, "Henry!"

It was partly his fault. He could've done a spell, too, or

taken back his horn. It seemed he managed the dark energy better.

Moris hesitated. To his left, a swirl of dust. To his right, a rolling bush. "Where am I?" he asked out loud. He was standing on a road, alone in a desert, clutching the blue horn.

"*Damn* it," he howled, staring at the horn. He raised his arm to toss it away; then, a thought struck him. He ground his teeth in frustration. He couldn't get rid of it—it was the only way to get back to Dantus.

He clenched the horn, face reddened in anger, and cast, "Itenelum, Dantus." He repeated, "Itenelum, Dantus."

Nothing. The horn wasn't activating.

He headed down the road. The radiant sun beat down. He hoped to return to where he had suffered the strangest experience he'd ever had.

In the distance, metal clattered. He raised his burned face, eyes squinting at the smudge on the horizon, and eyed a billboard. The advertisement promised *Coffee Cheer, Morning Cheers.*

He gasped, widening his eyes. "The sign."

He hastened to the billboard, looking for the dirt road. He stopped, and his face dropped again. No dirt road, only bushes. He sprinted to the bushes and yanked several from the ground. "Where is the road?"

How can he get back to the cabin? There was no dirt road to lead him.

Moris walked a few paces away from the bushes, his hands dirty and bleeding. Now he thought of getting home. But had his family survived? Or, they disappeared as well?

He walked toward his house, his weary feet dragging on the ground.

He reviewed his experience and sensed ominous times ahead. As if the ones he'd already lived through weren't enough.

Soon, the hum of a motor approached as an old pickup drove towards him. *Finally.* Covered in dust, he waved the vehicle down as he tucked the horn in his jacket.

The driver squinted at him and slowed to a halt. He backed up and addressed Moris. The driver was bald, with wrinkles on his forehead and a white beard. He rolled down the window and asked, frowning, "Hey boy, what are you doing here alone? Where's your family?"

Moris couldn't find words to respond.

"Do you want a ride?" The driver asked.

"Yes, please. I have been walking for hours and have no cell phone."

"Where're you headed?"

Anywhere out of here, Moris thought. "Near Austin," he said with a forced smile.

"Hop in. I'm going that way."

"Thank you very much, sir."

The clock on the dashboard flashed a useless twelve o'clock, and the radio was off. Moris hesitated to ask about the date; a scruffy boy on the side of the road asking that sounded normal, right? He remained silent.

The driver held a one-sided conversation that Moris mostly ignored. He stared out the window, his hand on the horn in his pocket and his mind on Henry and what he did with the wicked horn. The driver kept chattering.

When they finally arrived at the outskirts of Austin, he asked the driver to drop him off near his house. He got out and, embarrassedly, offered only a thank-you. He had no money.

He hesitated a second in trepidation after the pickup left him, then rushed toward home.

There were no cars in the house.

"Oh, *no*," he wailed. He feared death had visited his family.

Moris approached the door and rang the bell. No one answered. He searched for the hidden key below the flowerpot—it was still there—and went inside.

"Mom? Maya? Are you here?"

No one answered. He glanced around and sighed, smiling. He saw a picture of them. They still lived in the house.

He needed to figure out the date. He hurried to a laptop, opened it, and waited for it to boot up.

It said four twenty PM. He was about to click the clock to see the date when a door opened.

"Mom? Maya?" Moris replied, his voice shaky.

Susan and Maya entered, laden with grocery bags. The bags dropped when they saw Moris.

"Moris!" Susan cried. "You're alive."

She rushed and gave him an enormous hug.

"Moris, we missed you!" Maya said, joining the hug.

"Are you alright? What happened to you? Where's Henry?" Susan asked through her tears. "You disappeared for a year — we thought you were dead."

Moris yanked back, aghast. "A year?"

What had been a few weeks in the other dimension had been an entire year on Earth.

AUTHOR

I, **HECTOR CANTU KALIFA,** live in Monterrey, Mexico with my wife and my four children, two boys and two girls. I meditate every day, and I enjoy sports, so I exercise at least four times a week.

The Horn's Hoax: The Forbidden Instrument is my debut novel and Book One of the series The Horn's Hoax.

The writing of this book has been an unexpected pleasure for me, as I would never have imagined myself writing a book.

It all began in September 2019. It was intended to be a ten-page short story. But as I wrote, my imagination and my taste for writing kept me working. I realized on a blank page; I could create amazing things and let my imagination fly. Words kept coming, and I discovered the hard work of building a story; that's why it took me too long for this first book. With the help of many people, I gave my heart to create my first Art. So I hope this story reaches all the readers who enjoy fantasy. And for that, **I encourage you to leave a review. It will help me as an author, and I promise to look at it.**

If you would like to receive a high-quality image of the horns, Zadkiel's book, or the logo of the seven divines, send me an email—or tag me on social media— with a picture of my book.

To learn more about the release date of Book Two, or join the mailing list, visit www.hectorcantuk.com

I'm also on Twitter and Instagram @hectorckalifa_author